THE OTHER FRANK

When Detective Frank Vandegraf hears of the unexpected death of his ex-wife, he travels to the tiny rural town of Easton to face the demons of his past. But it's no respite from the challenging urban crimes of his regular job. No sooner has he arrived than two bizarre, violent deaths occur, and he feels irresistibly drawn to help unravel a web of mystery and intrigue. However, he's out of his jurisdiction, obstructed by officials, and amidst folk hiding their own secrets . . .

*Books by Tony Gleeson
in the Linford Mystery Library:*

NIGHT MUSIC
IT'S HER FAULT
A QUESTION OF GUILT

TONY GLEESON

THE OTHER FRANK

Complete and Unabridged

LINFORD
Leicester

First published in Great Britain

First Linford Edition
published 2017

A catalogue record for this book is available
from the British Library.

ISBN 978–1–4448–3131–3

Published by
F. A. Thorpe (Publishing)
Anstey, Leicestershire

Set by Words & Graphics Ltd.
Anstey, Leicestershire
Printed and bound in Great Britain by
T. J. International Ltd., Padstow, Cornwall

This book is printed on acid-free paper

To Annie, who has never left

1

'Do you mean to tell me, Frank, that you are actually taking some of your vacation time? Am I dreaming here?'

Detective Frank Vandegraf looked across the cluttered desk at his Lieutenant, Hank Castillo, and shrugged. 'Technically, Lou, I'm taking personal time, not vacation time. But yeah. Is there a problem?'

'A problem?' Castillo mused, a bit of a smile twitching the corners of his mouth. 'No, of course not. I'm just not sure I heard you right. You pretty much never take your time, Frank. It's actually become a bit of a problem with Personnel, just how much you've accrued. Are you feeling all right?'

Frank reached up to rub the back of his neck and then stopped himself. He was constantly being kidded about that involuntary gesture. 'I'm fine. It's just that I need to go out of town for a few days. A funeral and all that kind of thing.'

'Somebody close to you, I assume?'

'My ex-wife, Muriel.'

'Oh yes.' Castillo nodded. 'I remember her. I'm sorry. Was it unexpected?'

'Apparently she had an accident. They called me this morning. Small town in the Midwest.'

'I get the impression you hadn't stayed very close with her all these years.'

'Um . . . no. She moved back to her hometown, met some guy there and remarried. Hadn't heard from her in years.' There was an awkward silence. Frank shrugged. 'And clearly I won't after this either.'

'Maybe this is a good thing to be doing, then. Sounds like you decided you need to go, huh?'

Frank nodded, lips pursed. 'Yeah, well . . . I just figured, well, I've got the time and all.'

Castillo continued to nod sagely. He was a muscular man, whose thick eyebrows and mustache and graying temples all lent him an air of gravitas. As usual he had his suit jacket off but could still look dapper in shirt, tie, and vest. He looked down at the forms Frank had handed him. 'So you're departing tomorrow?'

'Got a flight out first thing. I'll be back next week.'

'Works for me, Frank. Good luck. You have a few things open, I believe.'

'Nothing really pressing anyway, just some pain in the neck re-canvasses and so forth. I'm happy to hand them off if you'd like.'

'I think that's wise. Unless I'm mistaken, Morrison is up right now.'

Frank suppressed a smile. Both he and Castillo understood that Detective Marlon Morrison was almost always unoccupied. He was just gifted that way. 'I'll put the stuff together for him, no problem.'

'All right, then,' Castillo said, looking anxious to return to his own workload. 'My condolences on your loss, Frank. Have a safe trip.'

'Yeah,' he said. 'Thanks.'

★ ★ ★

If Frank had been asked to rate his coping skills, he probably would have given himself reasonable marks. He would figure that he met whatever life threw at him with a fair amount of equanimity.

But there were several things he especially disliked and with which he did not necessarily cope all that well. One of these was flying. He avoided it whenever possible. In this case, it was unavoidable. With one stopover, he wound up spending over four hours in a cramped airline seat between two large seatmates before finally and mercifully deplaning.

Frank normally did like to drive. Driving offered a time he could use to let his mind work out problems, mull over cases and look for new solutions. Often he would suddenly realize he had been driving on 'automatic pilot' for long periods of time while he had gotten lost in his labyrinths of thought. He had about a two hour drive in his rental car from the airport to his final destination, but found he really had nothing to mull over at the moment.

Surprisingly he found himself bored and uncomfortable as he drove.

This entire trip, he anticipated, was going to be uncomfortable.

The Interstate highway would only take him so far before he had to exit and take local roads. Just outside of the town of Easton, he pulled into a small gas station to fill up. There were two pumps under a metal canopy in front of a garage and mini-market, with a sign that read RALPH'S AUTOMOTIVE SERVICES.

Another sign declared, PLEASE DO NOT SERVE YOURSELF GAS. WAIT FOR ATTENDANT. Frank found this rather refreshing, given that almost all the stations he encountered back home were self-service and largely automated.

Even finding a live breathing cashier was sometimes an impossible dream. Some states, he considered, had laws prohibiting self-dispensing of fuel. Maybe this was one of them.

He didn't have long to wait before a graying, haggard-looking soul in a cover-all and baseball cap strolled out from the garage, wiping his hands on a rag, and approached his window. The guy nodded to Frank and said nothing.

'Regular, please,' Frank said. 'Fill it up.' He fumbled around under the dashboard of the rental car to find the gas tank release and popped it. The guy nodded again and reached for one of the pumps.

Frank got out to stretch his legs while the gas pumped. He noted that the guy made no offer to check the oil or wipe the windshield. Those days were long, long gone.

'How far to Easton?' he asked the guy. He noted his coverall had the name RALPH stitched over the pocket.

'You're almost there. Another mile. Visiting?'

'Sort of. Come for a funeral, actually.'

Ralph nodded, a strange twitchy kind of nod, knitting his bushy eyebrows. 'Sorry for your loss. Hardly anybody comes this way who isn't a local.'

'You all do seem a little off the beaten track here. You the owner?'

Ralph nodded again. 'That would be me.'

'Lived here all your life?'

The man smiled at some private joke. He shook his head, again with that strange twitchiness. 'Not yet.' A wise guy, okay.

A thought occurred to Frank. 'Hey, I need to find some cigars for someone I'm going to see. You wouldn't happen to sell any, would you?'

'Sorry. Not something I stock. Used to love them, myself. Gave up smoking a while back.' Again he shook his head and smiled at some private joke. 'Best place to find decent cigars is at the gift shop in the motel in Easton. Likely you'll be staying there.'

'The Sportsman? That's where I've got a reservation.'

'Only lodgings in Easton, in fact. Good general store.'

As the guy finished up pumping the gas and extracted the pump, Frank couldn't help staring at him for a long moment.

There was something vaguely familiar about him but he couldn't place it. He was fairly nondescript: average height and build, maybe in his late fifties. The eyes, the mouth. The way he stood. Something.

The guy looked up at him. 'Something wrong?'

Frank shook it off. 'Naw, you just looked kinda familiar for a second.

Couldn't be anything. You ever been West?'

Ralph shook his head. 'Nope. Don't think you and I have ever had the pleasure, mister.'

Beneath his baseball cap, his eyes were a rather piercing clear gray. Again that little involuntary motion of his head.

'Oh, I'm sure we haven't. I've never been around here before.' Frank looked at the pump and pulled out his wallet. 'You take plastic?'

'Sure,' Ralph said, taking a credit card from Frank. 'Be right back, I'll go run this.'

Frank decided to check out the convenience store, so he got out of the car and followed him in. He selected a candy bar and some gum and told Ralph to put it on the card as well.

'Is the Sportsman comfortable?' Frank asked, just to have something to say.

'Yep,' Ralph smiled as he swiped Frank's card through the machine and keyed in the information of the transaction

'Decent restaurant, cocktail lounge.

You'll be comfortable there.'

'I wouldn't mind a good meal. I'm not much of a drinker these days.'

'Me neither. Kind of put the plug in the jug a while back. Don't drink, don't smoke. Don't know that I'll live longer but it'll sure seem that way.' Ralph handed a receipt to Frank for his signature and then exchanged the signed copy for the customer copy. 'Thank you, hope you have a nice visit.'

'As nice as coming for a funeral can be,' muttered Frank as he turned to leave the counter.

'One thing I've learned is certain,' Ralph said. 'Maybe the only thing.'

'I'm sorry, what's that?' Frank asked, stopping.

'Death, I mean.' Ralph shrugged. 'It's a constant, isn't it? For all of us?'

'I can't argue with that,' Frank allowed and continued to his car.

Strange guy. A little uncomfortable. Every word seemed to be an effort coming out of him. He still couldn't figure out why he seemed familiar. Frank somehow got some mixed messages from him, simultaneously looking for conversation but pushing him off. He seemed a very laid-back friendly sort at heart, but there was that underlying nervousness, that withdrawal.

Oh well. Small town. Different mindset and all that. He hoped everyone he met here wasn't like that. It didn't help his apprehensive mood one bit. Frank started up the car and pulled back onto the road.

★　★　★

The Sportsman's Lodge and Inn wasn't half bad, Frank had to admit. It was clean and well maintained, and he didn't mind the decor, which went heavy on wood paneling with a hunting motif: framed reproductions of hunting scenes and even two glassy-eyed stuffed deer heads.

The inn was a two-story complex, the ground floor of the main building taken up by the lobby, a restaurant, a gift/souvenir shop, and a convenience store. The woman behind the counter was outgoing and smiling as she signed Frank in, handed him his key and gave him directions to the room.

'Let me know if you have any questions, Mr. Vandegraf. Are you here to visit family?'

'In a manner of speaking,' he said, taking the key. 'I'm here for a funeral.'

'Oh my gosh,' she said. 'You must mean Muriel Lansdowne.'

'That would be her.'

'I'm so sorry. Terrible thing. Such a nice lady, to die in such a way.'

'I'm told she had an accident? Fell off a ladder, something of that nature?'

The woman nodded gravely. She was perhaps fifty, rusty brown hair sprinkled with just a touch of gray, with large earnest eyes behind rimless glasses. 'Darnedest thing. Her husband came home and found her on the ground. It seems she was trying to get a birds' nest out of a gutter of their house, or some such.'

'Darnedest thing,' Frank agreed.

'Poor Francis. I guess you know him, right? Such a nice fellow. He was heartbroken.'

'I don't really know him all that well,' Frank admitted. 'I suppose I'll get to know him this week.'

'So you're a relative of Muriel's? She didn't talk much about her immediate family but I thought they were mostly gone.'

'We used to be married. She and I hadn't talked in some years.'

'Oh. I see. Well, my condolences, I'm sorry for your loss. We all liked Muriel very much. She was a very helpful soul, always reaching out to help others.'

'That sounds like her, all right.' Frank smiled wanly at the woman and waved his key on its old-fashioned plastic fob. 'I'll go park by the room and check it out now. Thank you.'

It only took him a few minutes to decide the room would be quite satisfactory and to unpack his bag. The bed seemed comfortable, the television seemed to work, and he planned to only be sleeping and killing a small amount of time here. The room was furnished in similar fashion to the lobby: wood paneling, a couple of framed hunting prints. He was disappointed there was no glassy-eyed deer head on the wall to watch over him while slept. Next he could check out the motel shops for the cigars and then perhaps try the restaurant. He also realized he had forgotten a few toiletries — he wasn't accustomed to travel. Well, undoubtedly he could find stuff like toothpaste in the store as well. He locked up and walked back to the lobby.

The most direct route to the stores from Frank's room was to retrace his steps and go through the lobby. The chatty woman behind the counter was already gone, replaced by a solemn-looking young man reading a magazine. He looked up and smiled at Frank as the door opened and tinkled.

'Changed shifts already?' Frank asked, nodding at the young man.

'Oh, you mean Marge? She just went to take care of a customer in the gift shop. Anything I can help you with?'

'No thanks. Actually that's where I'm heading as well. I understand you have cigars there?'

'Oh sure. We're licensed to sell package goods as well, if you want. Save you a trip down the road.'

'Package goods? Oh. You mean like liquor. Alcohol.' Frank had heard the term but it was not in common usage in his part of the country. The young man nodded, still smiling. His expression was slightly less glazed than the deer behind him. 'Not really interested, but thanks. How's your restaurant?'

'Pretty good. I think tonight's special is pork chops.'

'That would be okay, but maybe I should go light. There might well be food tonight at the gathering I'm going to. I'm mostly interested in something like a sandwich to tide me over.'

'Oh yeah, no problem, plenty of sandwiches and stuff like that.' The glazed but happy smile never left his face as he returned his attention to the magazine.

Frank envied people who could be that happy all the time.

The store was clearly divided into two segments, the gift shop and convenience store, each with their own cashier stand. There was one lone customer in the gift store, a guy in a windbreaker, selecting a handful of cigars out of a box in a display.

'Those are a pretty good brand, I take it?' Frank asked as he walked up to the gent inspecting the smokes. The guy seemed startled and turned his head to Frank. He had a ruddy goatee and thick-rimmed glasses under a large wool newsboy cap. Wiry reddish hair stuck out from underneath. He seemed momentarily surprised before finally answering.

'I like 'em,' he shrugged.

'I don't know much about this stuff. Just buying a box for someone.' Frank reached over and found an unopened box, briefly inspected the package, and decided it'd do. He followed the guy back to the cash register, where Marge stood waiting for them, looking almost eager.

Obviously they weren't getting too many customers at the moment.

Funny, thought Frank, now *this* guy looks familiar to me. Something about the eyes. Is this what happens when you're in a strange place a thousand miles from home? Everyone starts looking familiar to you?

The guy had already laid a few other articles on the counter: a magazine, mouthwash, aerosol shaving cream. He said, 'I got these over there in the other part of the store. It's okay if I pay for these all right here, isn't it?'

'You bet,' Marge smiled. 'No problem at all.'

He pointed to the sparse rows behind her, where a small variety of liquor bottles were shelved. 'I'd also like a bottle of that bourbon there.' She reached back and grabbed a fifth of an off-brand Frank had never heard of.

'Do I need to see some ID for that alcohol?' Marge asked seriously. The guy hesitated. She broke out in a laugh. 'I'm just kidding, of course, Mr. Fields. You're not all that old, but surely you're over twenty-one!'

The guy instantly relaxed and shared a self-conscious laugh with her. 'Yeah, it's been a while since I got proofed. I should be flattered, shouldn't I?'

That reminded Frank of what else he needed. He laid the box of cigars on the counter and walked through to the convenience-store side, where he easily found a tube of toothpaste and a small bottle of shampoo. By the time he returned to Marge at the counter, the other guest was already hustling out the door with a bag under his arm.

'Find everything you need, Mr. Vandegraf?'

'I think so, thanks.'

'Interesting word that Mr. Fields used there, 'getting proofed.' They don't call it that around here. The kids usually refer to it as being 'carded'. I guess in Florida they use that expression.'

She rang up the total.

'So he's from Florida?' Frank asked absently as he dug out his wallet and extracted some bills. This lady was like the town crier, he reflected.

'Yep. Mr. Fields also just arrived last night, from Ocala, Florida. He's in the room two doors over from you.'

'Maybe he's here for the funeral too,' Frank said as he took his change from Marge. 'We might see each other tonight.'

'I don't know, he didn't say much when he checked in. If you're going to the funeral parlor tonight for Muriel's wake, will you be needing directions?'

She bagged up Frank's purchases and handed the paper package to him.

'As a matter of fact, sure.'

'The Theodore Rollins Funeral Home, straight down the main road here about a mile and turn right on West Elm.'

West Elm? How big was this town anyway? Whatever. He thanked her and started to leave, then he stopped and turned around again.

'Did you know Muriel very well?'

'Pretty well, I guess. Easton isn't a very big place. We all know each other. Her family's lived here for generations. I knew her parents too.'

'Tell me about her.'

'Well, both parents have passed on. They left her their house, that's where she and her husband live . . . I mean, where she *did* live. No living relatives that I know of.'

'Was she happy?'

'I'm not sure what you mean, Mr. Vandegraf.'

'Did she seem happy? Living here? Her life?'

'Why . . . yes. She was very outgoing, very sociable. She seemed to like everybody in town. She was active in all sorts

18

of clubs and things.'

'She and her husband . . . got along well?'

'I should say so. They seemed very happy together. He seems a very nice man.'

'I'm glad to hear that.'

'She was always so interested in other people. She liked playing matchmaker when she would find someone who seemed lonely to her. And you know, she loved to play detective.'

Marge smiled just a bit at that.

'Play detective? Now I'm not sure what you mean, Mrs . . . '

'Oh, just call me Marge. She was a great fan of mysteries . . . books, movies, television. She would joke about anything that came up that seemed to be a mystery. We'd kid her. Remember that TV show about the police detective's wife who solved crimes, Mrs. whatever it was?'

Frank nodded.

'She loved to watch reruns of that. We'd kid her she was like that wife, or maybe like that other character who's an elderly author and she stumbles over murders all the time? Anyway, we used to kid her about being like that.' She waved a hand. 'Of course, there was never anything like a murder around here. The only crimes around here are pretty tame. But she was always curious about people, joked about them having mysterious skeletons in their closet and things like that.'

'Yes,' Frank nodded. 'That sounds like her all right.'

'In fact she was once married to a policeman, I understand.'

'That's true. She was.'

'Oh my goodness. Of course. You're him, right? I mean . . . '

Frank smiled. 'I'm the policeman.'

'I feel so stupid. You told me earlier you were married to her. Of course you're the policeman. A real detective!'

'In real life,' Frank offered, 'being married to a detective isn't always that great, Marge. There are things that are beyond solving, I guess.' He nodded his goodbye and headed out the door.

He dropped the items in his room and returned to the restaurant. A turkey sandwich and coffee filled him up adequately.

There were still a few hours to kill before the service at the funeral home. He figured he'd flop out on the bed, maybe catch a nap, or watch some television. He was back in his room, sitting on the bed, removing his shoes, when the knock came at the door.

He opened it to a paunchy guy with thinning blond hair and a rather pleasant expression.

Frank looked at him expectantly. 'Yes?'

'You must be Frank,' the guy said, smiling tentatively.

'I must be, you're right. Let me guess. You must be the other Frank, right?'

The visitor extended his hands as if in surrender, with a shy smile. 'I always heard you were some detective. But it's Francis, actually.' He still looked hesitant. They had never met in person, and Frank knew they'd both be apprehensive about how awkward this meeting was going to be.

Frank stepped back into the room. 'Come on in, Francis.' He offered a hand and they shook.

Francis's grip was firm, Frank noted.

Nothing tentative there.

'I figured you'd be here, and that it might be a good idea to come over and introduce myself.' He looked around self-consciously and Frank gestured him to sit down in the only chair, sitting himself back on the bed.

'Nice of you. How have you been holding up?'

Francis shrugged, looking down and distant. 'About as good as I could expect, I guess. This was one hell of a shock.'

'I'm sure it was. I'm sorry for your loss.'

'Nice of you to come, Frank. I appreciate it.'

Frank just nodded. There was an awkward silence. The two men both gazed around the room trying to think of the next thing to say. Finally Frank reached over and picked up the box of cigars he had bought and extended it to Francis.

'I remember hearing you were a lover of cigars. Muriel happened to mention it the last time we spoke, a year or two ago. I thought I'd . . . well, just to let you know there's no hard feelings on my part.'

Francis, surprised, took the box. He just stared at it for a long moment before looking up. 'Wow. This is really nice of you.'

'Sorry, I didn't get to, you know, wrap it or anything.'

'No no, this is great. Just great.'

'I hope the brand's to your liking. I have to admit I'm kind of ignorant about them.'

Francis hefted the box up and down. 'Oh yeah, this is great.' He shook his head. 'Wow. This means a lot. You know, when I came over here, I wasn't sure how this was gonna play out.'

'I understand.'

'I mean, Muriel coming back here and marrying me and all . . . '

'No, I get it. Everything's okay, Francis. I get the impression you were really good to her and she was happy. She deserved that.'

Francis looked lost in thought for another long moment. 'She never said anything bad about you, you know. No blame or stuff like that.'

'It just didn't work out. It's not easy being a cop's wife. We have lots of divorces in the department. Never any time for her. Always bringing home dreadful garbage. Stuff I couldn't share with her, or anybody else for that matter.'

'But she loved the whole idea of being a detective,' Francis smiled. 'Loved the books and the TV shows.'

'I know. She got me interested in them too. I still watch some of those shows, read some of those books. When I have the time. Which isn't all that often.'

'She said you'd watch with her or read something she told you about so you could tell her how unrealistic it was. How police work wasn't like that.'

That made Frank smile, almost laugh. 'That's still why I like them. Sometimes I wish things were as easy as in those stories. It entertains me.'

'Muriel really liked other people. She lived to socialize and try to help people out.'

'Yeah, that sounds right. I'm glad she found a life where she could do all that. Our life was kind of stifling for her.'

They talked a few more minutes, the conversation remaining stilted and jerky. Francis talked about what their life in Easton had been like. Finally Frank broached the subject of her death.

'So, what exactly happened to Muriel, anyway?'

Francis took a long moment to compose his thoughts. 'It was a freak accident. I had closed up the store early. When I got home, she wasn't in the house. I went around looking for her, and . . . well, I found her. Outside. On the ground next to the ladder. Her neck was broken. It was awful, just awful. I ran inside and called 911 but she was . . . well, she was already gone.' He had to pause to regain some composure. 'Damnedest thing. I don't understand why she would go up on that ladder by herself. Why couldn't she have waited for me to come back?'

'Why exactly was she up there to begin with?'

'There was a bird's nest in the gutter of the roof. She had mentioned it a couple of times. That's all I can think of.' Francis drooped his head and covered it with his hands for a long moment. He continued without changing the position, talking through his hands. 'She had been bugging me to get it down and move it to . . . someplace safe. I kept putting it off.'

'Francis, it wasn't your fault this happened. Even I can see that. Don't blame yourself.'

'She fell off the damned ladder. That's the explanation the paramedics from the fire department came up with. That's what the coroner said. She had gotten up on the ladder and she . . . just . . . fell . . . off.' Frank could tell he was beginning to cry behind those hands. 'Damnedest thing. Damnedest thing ever.'

Frank just waited it out. There really was nothing else he could say at that point. Well, just one.

'I'm sorry, Francis. I'm really, really sorry.'

Francis looked up, his eyes a bit red, and nodded, regaining his composure.

'Well, let me tell you how to get to the viewing tonight. It's over at the Rollins Funeral Home down the street.'

'Yeah, Marge in the lobby told me. Did

you say viewing?' Frank felt a little uneasy.

'It's closed coffin, but you know, these wakes, people still call it 'viewing hours.' There'll be some conversation about her, Father McNulty will say some prayers, stuff like that. Then there's a kind of reception, some food and stuff, conversation about Muriel. The funeral mass will be tomorrow morning at St. Dismas' Church, and then the burial. That's sort of how we do it around here. Some places, they have the get-togethers after the burial, but we're just more comfortable doing it the night before.'

Frank nodded. All this ritual over death made him uncomfortable. He figured it had to do with his own experience, having seen death up close so often. He found little in the way of comfort in religious or philosophical homilies. The familiar comforting rituals of food and socializing offered him little respite. Nothing could take away the starkness and finality he witnessed on a regular basis. It had been still another wedge between Muriel and himself.

'So, I guess I'll see you over there then?' Francis asked, standing up. Frank rose and shook his hand again.

'Sure. So, about seven?'

Francis nodded. He held up the box. 'And thanks again for these. I've considered giving up smoking, but . . . well, you know, old habits and all. And not a good week to be thinking about such things anyway.'

'You're right about that. One thing at a time.'

★ ★ ★

Driving through the town of Easton, Frank estimated there might be two or three thousand people at most living there. Muriel had grown up in Easton before moving west to attend college, get a job and meet Frank. After the divorce it was where she had instinctively returned. Probably everybody in town had known her.

The funeral home was full. He worked his way uncomfortably through endless introductions to neighbors and friends, explaining time and again his relation to her, and listening to innumerable variations on the theme of what a lovely woman Muriel had been and what a horrible tragedy that she was taken before her time. The coffin dominated the front of the room, covered in floral arrangements.

Frank noted with relief that it was indeed closed throughout the proceedings.

Folding chairs had been set up in front of the tableau. When the gathering was asked to take seats by the priest (Father McNulty, he assumed), Frank sought out Francis and sat beside him. After a few opening remarks, the good Father asked if anyone would like to come up and say anything about the deceased. Numerous red-eyed folks did just that, attesting to Muriel Lansdowne's kindness, good nature, and generosity. One middle-aged woman who introduced herself as Grace claimed to be 'Muriel's best friend in the world.'

'Why, it was only a few days ago,' Grace recounted, 'that Muriel was trying to find a nice lady for a local gentleman she knew who seemed lonely.'

Numerous heads bobbed up and down

in recognition. This activity had been an open secret, it would seem. 'That was her: always thinking of the other person, sensitive to their needs and their discomfort.'

Frank glanced over to note Francis' decidedly forced expression. Not only, it seemed, was he familiar with the details of the story but he did not share Grace's approval of Muriel's part in it. There had to be some story there. Small towns. He considered how much he wanted to get back to his urban comfort zone again.

Finally the train of well-wishers subsided and Father McNulty stood up and led the gathering in a decade of the rosary and a few other prayers.

Finally he made a few closing remarks and announced that there would be 'food and fellowship' in the adjoining hall. Everyone filed out, half solemn and half eager for the eating and talking to come. These strange customs we observe, Frank thought to himself. Let's cry, let's eat.

'I noticed your reaction to the remark about Muriel's matchmaking,' Frank murmured to Francis, mostly just to break the awkwardness, as they followed the line into the hall. Francis almost laughed aloud.

'I told her it was a bad idea. She had this interest in this guy, Ralph, he owns a filling station a way down the road. You might remember Muriel, she had this idea that everyone felt just the way she did, they all needed somebody in their lives.'

'Sounds familiar, yeah.'

'Well, my take is that Ralph just wants to be left alone. He moved here a couple, three years back, keeps to himself, I think he just wants to keep his own counsel, you know? Women don't seem to get that.'

Frank nodded. 'I actually met Ralph, stopped for gas. I got the impression he was a native.'

'Ralph? Naw. You mean you actually got more than a handful of words out of him?'

'Come to think of it,' Frank replied, 'no.'

A long table crammed with various cold cut meats and salads greeted them. They grabbed plates and dug in.

Conversation between them ebbed. There were a few tables to sit but most people, including Frank and Francis, simply stood and ate.

Several people approached to talk to Francis and offer their support, and to introduce themselves to Frank. After a while the talk around them had grown lively. That was the idea, Frank mused, behind gatherings such as this. 'Food and fellowship,' as the priest had called it, lifted the mood and brought the conversation around from the desolation of loss to happier cherished memories of the departed. It seemed to work. People would go home, if not exactly happy, at least not despondent.

The gathering began to break up around ten, and Frank accompanied Francis out to the parking lot.

There was something still nagging at Frank. Ralph Watkins had looked familiar to him, but he had dismissed the idea in the belief that Ralph had spent his life in this area, so they couldn't have possibly met. Now that he knew otherwise, that Ralph had in fact originally come from somewhere else, his curiosity was piqued. 'Tell me, Francis, any idea where this Ralph Watkins guy came from before he moved here?'

Francis looked reluctant to say anything, apparently in an internal debate over how to answer. Finally, stopped in front of his car, he said, 'Back east. He's from somewhere in New England.'

'He told you that?'

'No. Muriel figured it out. Ralph never talks about his past.'

'Muriel figured it out? What does that mean exactly?'

Another long pause before answering.

Francis was not sure he wanted to continue, and did so with some obvious reluctance.

'Like I said, she loved to play detective. She called Ralph the 'mystery man.' She — well, she called it putting some clues together. She figured she needed to know something about him to find him just the right girl.' He shook his head. 'Damn crazy woman.' He said it with surprising feeling, almost vehemence.

'Forgive me, Frank. I shouldn't speak

of the departed that way, certainly not someone I loved as much as her.'

'What exactly did she figure out about Ralph?'

'She went by the gas station one day and while Ralph was taking care of another customer, she stepped inside — you know, where his little soda store and cash register are? She saw a Boston newspaper tucked into his chair behind the counter. That's not something that's readily available around here. You have to go to some trouble to get one, maybe drive a ways to a newsstand in a bigger town like Springdale. She figured he was catching up on news from his home area.'

Something was tugging at the back of Frank's brain but he couldn't figure it out. He was still working it around when he heard the sirens.

Fire engines blared by, horns and sirens screaming, lights flashing frenetically. Everyone in the parking lot froze and turned to watch.

'Must be a good one,' Francis exclaimed. 'Looks like the whole blamed fire department is on its way!'

2

The Sportsman's Grill must have been a fairly popular restaurant because there were already a number of people seated and having breakfast when he entered it. Most of them were talking animatedly and the room buzzed with the conversations.

'Always this busy for breakfast?' he asked the young waitress who presented him a cup of coffee, a menu and a warm smile.

'Sometimes. This is a little more than usual. There's a funeral this morning, someone who was well known around here.'

Frank nodded. 'That is in fact why I'm here. Everybody seems pretty excited about something, is that because of the funeral?'

'No, probably the big explosion and fire last night. The word got out about that early this morning.'

Frank recalled the sirens from the evening before. 'Big fire, then? Anybody hurt?'

'Oh yeah. He died. The guy who owned the service station down the road.'

Frank almost dropped his menu. He did spill a little of his coffee.

'Ralph Watkins, you mean?'

'Why, yes!'

'Ralph Watkins died last night?'

'It was horrible. The gas pumps went up, the whole station. They're saying it was an accident. He set it off while he was smoking.'

'While he was smoking, you say?'

'That's what they're saying. Apparently Ralph . . . well, you wouldn't know him, right? You're not from around here?'

'That's correct, but I did meet him yesterday, in fact.'

'Well, apparently Ralph got a little drunk last night and tried to light up out front of his station and there was a leak somewhere, gas spilled on the ground or something like that, and . . . ' She opened her eyes wide. 'Poor guy.'

That couldn't be the right story. Frank

decided she had gotten her details wrong. Rumors were like that old game called Telephone: things changed as they passed from person to person until they had transmuted entirely. He was sure he'd hear more about this as the day went on.

'So,' the waitress continued, her smile returning, 'ready to order or do you need a minute?'

* * *

The small church of Saint Dismas was crowded for the service. Frank sat in the back and saw Francis in the front pew, looking drained and downcast. It was finally all hitting home for him. Frank was quite familiar with the process many loved ones went through in coming to grips with a loss — much more familiar than he had ever wanted to be.

The Mass went quickly for Frank as his mind spun throughout the service. Father McNulty offered more words in memory of the departed Muriel. Soon Frank found himself driving in the procession to the cemetery, where he joined the group congregating around the open grave.

The priest said some more prayers with obvious feeling, blessed the gathering, and left the final descent of the coffin into its gaping hole to the grave tenders.

Frank had still not had the chance all morning to approach Francis, who had continued to grow more haggard and morose-looking as the proceedings continued.

Now Frank hoped they'd have a chance to speak before they left the cemetery grounds. He walked across the stream of departing mourners towards Francis, who stood near the grave conversing earnestly with Father McNulty. The priest was looking down, his left ear to Francis, listening intently, and nodding at what was being said.

Frank began to have second thoughts that this was the moment to talk with Francis, but when he was a few steps away and hesitated, both men looked up and smiled at him. In Francis' case it was wan and weak, but it seemed welcoming.

Father McNulty motioned him towards them and extended a hand. 'I take it you must be Detective Vandegraf,' he said. 'It was good of you to come. I've heard a few things about you.' He was perhaps fifty, with a spark of merry intelligence in his eyes, and a deep voice tinged with a melodic Irish brogue.

'I hesitate to ask what those things might be,' Frank said, taking the priest's hand. 'Please, call me Frank, Father.'

'Kieran McNulty,' the priest replied, his smile growing. 'And I'd be pleased to have you call me simply Kieran, Frank. Take my word, the reputation that precedes you is admirable.'

'I can only hope that's the truth.'

'Believe me, neither Muriel nor Francis ever had an unkind word for you, lad.' He shrugged. 'The past is the past.' His grip was quite firm. Frank wondered if the good Father had once been a prizefighter or a longshoreman.

Francis continued to make an effort at smiling but it was obvious it was a fight. Frank turned to him and said, 'Sorry I didn't get the chance to speak with you at the service. How are you doing?'

'I guess everything hit me particularly

hard last night,' he replied. 'Maybe we can talk a little later. Will you be leaving soon or will we have a chance?'

'My flight's a redeye tonight. We can talk before then.'

Francis nodded.

'By the way,' Frank continued, 'I heard about the fire last night. Someone said it was Ralph Watkins, is that right?'

McNulty nodded gravely. He was still holding Frank's hand in his. 'A horrible thing.'

'The story I got was that he drank too much and tried to light a cigarette around his pumps. That can't be right.'

Finally letting go of Frank's hand, McNulty stared at him as he continued to nod. 'That is indeed the story I heard as well. Except it was a cigar, not a cigarette.'

'Something about that seems strange,' Frank said.

'Ralph was quite the cigar smoker,' Francis said hesitantly. 'And he used to be seen in the local bar all the time. Maybe it's not so strange.'

He turned to McNulty and extended

his own hand to shake.

'Thanks, Father, we'll talk later then?'

'Of course. Give me a call later on and we'll talk as we arranged.'

'Frank, forgive me, I gotta run.' He shook Frank's hand as well.

'Sure, Francis. I'll give you a call before I leave, or why don't you just come by the motel when you're free, okay? We really should talk before I leave.'

As Francis trudged away across the rolling grass of the cemetery, McNulty turned to Frank and his face grew more serious. 'Just what did you mean, that something seems strange?'

'Well, I didn't know this guy Ralph, of course, but I spoke with him when I stopped at his station on the way in yesterday. He told me he had given up smoking and drinking.'

McNulty nodded more vigorously. He paused a moment as if judging whether to go on and then said, 'I have to tell you, it struck me a bit odd as well. Can I confide something in you, relying upon your professional ethics as a police investigator, perhaps?'

'You're not going to divulge a confessional admission or anything like that?'

McNulty laughed. 'Oh, Lord no. That's a sacred bond, lad. The seal of the confessional is sacrosanct. Not to mention the man was not a churchgoer, much less to my church. No, but this has to do with a different kind of confidentiality. You see, Ralph and I shared a certain fellowship. Both of us had put the plug in the jug some while back.'

'He used that exact expression,' Frank said.

'We're both recovering alcoholics. Often were the times one of us would call the other for a bit of moral support in a rugged moment.'

'A twelve-step program?' Frank asked.

'An anonymous one, and we can only 'out' ourselves and not others; but with death that no longer applies.' He read Frank's expression. 'What, you think men of the cloth aren't susceptible to such maladies, now?'

'No, I don't think that one bit,' replied Frank. 'Not much surprises me, Padre. Not anymore.'

'Kieran, please. That Father stuff is appropriate in some cases but not here, all right, are we agreed? At any rate, I didn't know all that much about Ralph but I did know that after he moved here, he made the effort to clean up his life, and to my knowledge, the man had not touched a drop in at least a year. And as for the cigars — it was my understanding he had indeed given up smoking as well.'

'I suppose people do relapse.'

'Of course. Of course. But, Frank, I must tell you, it doesn't feel right in Ralph's case. Do you know the feeling when your gut just tells you something isn't right?'

'Oh, do I. I couldn't do my job if I didn't have that particular sense.'

'Well then, just between you and me, lad, the story doesn't feel right, and I am strongly inclined to the opinion there is more to this than I've heard so far.'

'Is it possible that you and I have heard twisted rumors? That the real story is something different?'

'I'd like to believe that, but the unfortunate truth is that I got the story from two of my parishioners, who happen to be a captain of the Fire Department and a dispatcher from the local Sheriff's Department. When they found Ralph's terribly burned body — and may he rest in eternal peace — there was part of a whiskey bottle beside him and there were shards of a cigar and the burned remains of a matchbook nearby as well. It was a foregone conclusion. Or so it would seem.'

'Are you saying you suspect that it wasn't an accident? That maybe this was all set up to look like it?'

McNulty extended his lower lip and looked thoughtful.

'Foul play? A bit dramatic. We're not in a television melodrama or a turgid whodunit book, are we now? Or back in your big bad city teeming with ill will?' At this he smiled again and winked mischievously.

'Still. You agree it's strange. Something isn't adding up here, is it?'

'Agreed. Perhaps it was an accident of a different sort.'

'What do you know about Ralph

Watkins anyway? I was told he only moved here a few years ago? That he kept to himself?'

'A closed book, that one. Wasn't of the tendency to let people in very close. He moved here about — oh, I'd say two, three years ago. Took over the station, which had been closed for some time, and got it running again. He was a good mechanic, ran a pretty decent business.'

'He didn't socialize much, I gather.'

'No, not at all. He was cordial enough to everybody, if a bit awkward. Struck me as above-average intelligent as well.'

'You seem to have gotten to know him?'

'Perhaps a bit more than others, once he started coming to our meetings. We'd have coffee together afterward now and then. He was awkward, as I said — uncomfortable with opening up. We discussed feelings and such now and then, for what they were worth. It was a slow process and still in progress.'

Despite himself, Frank felt the gears of his investigating mind kick in. Before he realized it he found himself jumping into the hunt. 'He wasn't the only mechanic in town, was he?'

'Oh no. There are two other mechanics around Easton. One runs the other gas station, on the other end of town. The other just fixes cars and such.'

'Might there have been a business rivalry, that sort of thing?'

McNulty waved the idea off with his hand. 'You're suggesting one of the other mechanics in town eliminated him? No, no. Both are decent lads I've known for many years now. And it's not as if any of them are hurting for business either. Everybody's got a car or a truck or one of each and there's plenty of business to go around. It's hardly a cutthroat industry in these parts. Back in your big city, do mechanics go around eradicating one another in violent manner?'

'More likely they're non-violently over-charging their customers,' Frank replied. 'You said you spoke to someone at the Sheriff's. How are the local police regarding this, as an accident?'

'It would seem, yes.'

'I'm thinking perhaps I need to go talk

to them, just air my misgivings before I leave. Do you feel strongly enough about it to do the same with me?'

McNulty considered that. 'I'm not sure, Frank. Let me think on that a bit. For now, it's just strange to me. I don't necessarily suspect foul play afoot or anything like that. But by all means, follow your own conscience on how you wish to proceed.'

The twinkle in McNulty's eye clued Frank that perhaps he wasn't as much the small-town cleric as he was enjoying playing the role of one. Frank asked directions to the Sheriff's station and they chatted a bit further before shaking hands and bidding one another goodbye.

★   ★   ★

The Freeman County Sheriff's Department was a long, low building with a decent sized parking lot. Double glass doors led into the station. A uniformed receptionist watched him approach as she sat at a gap in a glass wall at a high counter.

Before he was halfway to her, she said,

'Can I help you?'

Frank decided it wouldn't hurt to display his ID and badge and had it out at the ready. She gave him a polite smile as she looked it over.

'I was wondering if I could speak to whoever is dealing with last night's death of Ralph Watkins,' he said.

'The Sheriff's unavailable at the moment but you can speak with Deputy Maravich,' she said, staring blankly at him, vestiges of the polite but blank smile refusing to leave her face.

'That sounds like a good place to start,' Frank said. 'Thank you.'

She punched a number on her desk phone and spoke into her headset: 'There's a Detective Vanderbilt from out of town to see you about the Ralph Watkins accident. Okay, I'll tell him.' Then she pointed to the seats along the far wall of the reception area.

'He'll be right out, please take a seat, Detective Vanderbilt.'

'That's Vandegraf, actually,' Frank said. 'Thanks.' He strolled across the room to the benches and sat down, gazing around at the surroundings.

This couldn't be more different from the police station to which he was accustomed. It was quiet, modern, spacious, and nearly empty.

A tall, dark-haired, serious-looking uniformed man emerged from around a corner.

'Detective Vanderbilt?'

Frank hoisted himself to his feet again. 'That's Vandegraf. Frank Vandegraf.'

The deputy extended a hand. 'I'm Deputy Sheriff Lee Maravich. Nice to meet you. Why don't you come on back?' Frank detected a bit of a drawl.

Frank followed the deputy back around the same corner, down a corridor and into a large room that was divided up into about a dozen cubicles. Now Frank could hear familiar sounds: phones ringing, computer noises, the murmur of voices.

Maravich stepped into one of the cubicles and motioned for Frank to take one of the seats facing the desk.

Once they were both seated, Frank went through the ritual again of showing his badge and credentials and briefly explained his reason for being there. Maravich said, 'So you're here about Ralph Watkins too, huh? Must be something going on with that whole thing.'

'Excuse me?' Frank asked.

'The Sheriff is in with two somber sorts right now, also from out of town,' Maravich said. 'What, are you guys coming in on buses to talk about Ralph?'

'I've got nothing to do with them,' Frank said, extending his hands.

Maravich sat back in his swivel chair. 'So what specifically brings you here anyway?'

Frank explained why he had come to Easton in the first place and gave a bit of his own background, then laid out the misgivings he harbored about the story he had heard behind the death of Ralph Watkins.

Maravich listened carefully, an earnest expression on his face.

'I realize I don't know that much about the man,' Frank summed up his explanation, 'but there's something that just didn't ring true to me about this. I figured it couldn't hurt to come forward and just tell you about my conversation with Watkins yesterday. I might possibly have been the last person to speak with him while he was still alive.'

Maravich nodded and seemed lost in thought for several seconds. 'So Ralph told you he had given up drinking and smoking.'

'That's right.'

'You have to admit, that's not an awful lot to go off of, sir. Even if he did say that, people do say things that might not be true. Maybe he wanted people to *think* he had stopped drinking and smoking, if you get my meaning?'

'That's not out of the question,' Frank allowed. 'But it was odd that he would bring it up to me. I was a stranger, passing through. Why mention it at all? Why bother convincing me either way? Why would he even care what I thought?'

Maravich shrugged. 'It is odd, I'll give you that.'

'All I'm saying is that maybe he didn't just get drunk and set his station on fire. I'm just a visitor here, I'm leaving for home tonight, and of course it's your case. I just wanted to have my observations on the record, for you to be able to consider that.'

'And I appreciate that, Detective . . . Vandegraf?' Frank nodded. 'I'm sorry for your loss. I've known Francis and Muriel for a while now. She was a very nice lady.'

Frank took out one of his business cards and handed it to the deputy. 'I'm at the Sportsman Lodge if you need to reach me today, and my cell phone is on my card. I'm heading back tonight.'

Maravich's phone buzzed and he picked up the receiver, muttering a few terse 'Uh-huh's and hanging up. 'Forgive me, we have a situation I have to move on right away.' He rose and shook Frank's hand, looking suddenly hurried.

'I understand, Deputy Maravich. Thanks for your time. I can find my way out.'

'Appreciate that. Have a safe journey home. Oh, by the way?'

'Yes, Deputy?'

'I place you now. Once or twice Muriel mentioned you in passing. That she had previously been married to a police detective.'

'Huh. I hope it wasn't all bad.'

'As a matter of fact, I do not recall anything bad. She was almost proud of you, I got the impression once.'

Frank shrugged. How about that.

In the lobby on his way out, Frank noted a heavy-set man that he figured was the Sheriff, uniformed, talking earnestly with a man and a woman in buttoned-up dark suits. They seemed out of place here. To Frank they looked a lot like Federal agents he had known. It looked as if this was quite the busy place today. All three, with solemn expressions, shot him a glance as he passed.

* * *

Check-out time was still a couple of hours away but Frank figured he'd pack up and spend the time with Francis before the drive back to the airport for his late flight home. Francis did not answer his phone so he left a message when voice mail cut in. Frank figured Francis had met up with the priest as they had been discussing earlier.

Apparently everything had finally hit Francis emotionally and he was in need of some spiritual and psychic support. He hoped they'd have the chance to have another conversation before he had to depart. He quickly packed and laid out on the bed to watch television to bide a little time.

Evidently he was still tired or the bed was inordinately comfortable; he drifted off and suddenly found himself being roused from his catnap by a knocking on his door. He rose to open it.

'Deputy Maravich. Fancy seeing you here.'

'Detective Vandegraf. Got a minute for a few words?'

'Sure, come on in. Don't tell me you already decided to pursue the question of Ralph Watkins further?'

'Actually, no,' Maravich said as he stepped into the room. Frank motioned him to the lone chair where Francis Lansdowne had sat the evening before. 'The Sheriff seems satisfied that it was an accident. This is in fact a different matter. Marge Palmer up at the front tells me you had a conversation with another guest here last night, a Barry Fields?'

'Barry, that's his first name?' The lyrics 'Straw Barry Fields Forever' suddenly started playing in his brain. 'I wouldn't call it a conversation. We exchanged some brief words in the gift shop. He wasn't a very talkative fellow.'

Maravich nodded. He pulled out a smart phone and keyed up a photo. 'Would this be the man you spoke with last night?'

Frank looked at a close-in shot of a man's face. He was very familiar with this kind of photo. He took them often himself.

'This man is dead. You took this at the scene of the death?'

Maravich nodded. His hand shook slightly as he held up the phone. Frank took the phone from him and looked more closely.

'This was your 'situation' a while ago, I take it.'

'Is he the man you spoke with last night?' Maravich repeated, looking concerned.

Frank stared at the photo silently for a long moment. 'He's different. Last night he had a beard, a goatee rather.' He made a gesture around his mouth with his fingers. 'And he had glasses. His hair was more ruddy. But ... yes. The facial structure is right. I'd say this is the same guy.' He handed the phone back to the deputy. 'What happened?'

'He was found dead in his car on the highway about ten miles away. Somebody shot him.'

'You gotta be kidding!'

'No, sir, I am not. Looks as if he was driving out of town early this morning, maybe around four. He was shot in the head, after which his car drove into the piling of an overpass.'

Frank shook his head. This was more insane than the things he had to regularly deal with back home.

'You're sure it's the same man?' Maravich asked again.

Frank nodded.

'Pretty sure. The nose, the eyebrows. The physiognomy of the face. His hair looks to be a different color but it's the same texture.'

Maravich smiled ruefully.

'Sounds like you're good police, as they say. Marge couldn't make a definite ID. She thought it wasn't the same guy.'

'No, it's the same guy, but he clearly went to some effort to change his appearance all of a sudden.'

Something began to stir in the back of his mind. 'He had identification, I suppose? And he must have had something to bring you back here — a receipt from the motel?'

The deputy nodded. 'He had a Florida driver's license and a credit card in the name of Barry Fields. His receipt from the Sportsman was on the seat next to him.'

'He was leaving town in the dead of night,' Frank murmured, searching his brain. What was bugging him? There was something . . .

'He must have flown in; the car was a rental from the airport, we learned that already. But it looks like he wasn't planning on flying out again. He was heading in the wrong direction, for one thing, and we haven't found plane tickets or anything like that yet. Maybe he was going to drive home to . . . I think it's Ocala?'

A sudden connection virtually exploded in Frank's head all at once. He thought he remembered why the guy had looked familiar. He wasn't positive but . . .

'I don't think his real name is Barry Fields,' Frank said. 'And I don't think he was really from Florida.'

'What are you saying, Detective?'

'If what I suspect is true, this guy's name is Artie.' He spent another few seconds lost in thought. 'Artie Burns. At least that's the name I know him by.'

'Artie Burns.' Maravich stared at Frank. 'Who's that and why do you think that?'

'It's the look in his eyes when we talked. It just hit me this instant, why I was so sure he looked familiar. Back home, we once picked him up on suspicion. Questioned him and had to let him go when he lawyered up.'

Maravich's eyes got bigger. This must be like listening to a fairy tale for him, Frank figured.

'Burns was — I guess you'd call him a fixer. He would travel around to look after the interests of the organization back East.

Clean up messes. Or so we believed.'

'You mean, he was like a hit man,' Maravich said.

'He was a person of interest in a suspicious death. The victim was a local businessman we suspected of running some schemes and might have run afoul of some out of town interests. We don't like wise guys in our city to begin with but we *really* don't like it when carpetbaggers come in to get a foot in the door, do things like murders for hire. We found this guy about to head to the airport. I was one of two detectives who questioned him. He claimed he was a salesman making the rounds, and then all of a sudden this slick expensive lawyer showed up and popped him. His story stunk to us, but we couldn't hold him.'

Maravich was rapt at the story. He nodded thoughtfully. 'And you think this Barry Fields is the same guy, this Artie Burns? Why?'

'Like I said. It's the eyes. He looked different from this guy. His hair was different, he had no eyeglasses, and he had, like, this bushy mustache but otherwise he was clean-shaven. I was sitting across the table from him. The eyes, they were the same. The conversation wasn't all that long. He didn't talk much. But he would stare at us. Cold. Sizing us up every second, figuring his angle. We call it bad intent. Kind of unsettling, like a snake looking at a bird? When the guy you call Fields looked at me in the gift shop, I flashed on that stare, that look. It took me a while to place it, to put the circumstances and the name to it.'

'You were sure this guy Burns was the killer in your case?'

'We had that strong feeling. You probably know what I'm talking about.' Maravich nodded slowly. 'The death was made to look like an accident. The victim fell out of a window at a construction site late at night. It didn't make sense. And then this Burns guy turned up. He'd been in town for a day or two before the death and he was leaving immediately afterward. Really fishy. But we didn't have enough to hold him.'

'And you never cleared the case, am I right?'

Frank shook his head. 'We already had our eyes on the victim before he turned up dead. Not worth going into details here, but he was deep into all sorts of stuff. We were sure it was an arranged death. But we could never prove it.'

'How long ago was this?'

'Two and a half years ago.'

Maravich nodded again. 'We don't get a lot of investigations we can't close, but there have been a couple I was personally involved with, and I know how they particularly rankle.' Frank returned his knowing nod.

The deputy considered all this further before continuing. 'If you're right about this, then we've got some kind of organized crime thing here? That staggers the imagination, I've got to say. Why was the guy here, and how and why did he get killed? If this is at all possible, I'm totally at sea.'

'I'd like to be of some help to you here. I don't want to get in the way where I'm not wanted or anything, but . . . '

'I understand, Detective. In fact I wish you could hang around another day or two, be some help as a witness and a background source.' He stared at Frank for a long moment.

'I think I might be able to arrange that,' Frank said. 'Long as you're sure I'm welcome.'

★　★　★

'Frank, this is a surprise to hear from you. You're not back already?'

'Nope, I'm still in Easton. Lieutenant, I'm going to need to stay here for a little longer than I originally anticipated. Any problem with my taking a few more days?'

'Frank, you've got ridiculous amounts of time accrued, we both know that. What do you want me to tell you? Part of me could use you back, you certainly know that. Part of me is delighted to see you're finally taking some time off away from work, relaxing for a change.'

'Relaxing . . . yeah. Anyway, you're okay with that?'

'Sure. How long are you thinking?'

'I'm thinking staying over this weekend.

The earliest return flight I can get is Sunday — be back at work Monday?'

'I do think the unit can survive without you for a few more days, Frank. I would have expected you to take the weekend at very least anyway. Come back Tuesday.'

Castillo paused a moment in thought.

'Frank, I know you weren't all that close with your ex any more, but if you need some time for closure or whatever that you didn't anticipate, feel free to take whatever you need. As I said, you have it coming.'

Frank was about to tell him that wasn't the case, but thought better of it. The less said the better. In any case, he was touched by Castillo's unexpected show of support.

'Thanks, Lou. I should be fine coming back Tuesday.'

'Morrison won't be happy to have to carry your cases a few more days, but he'll survive.'

Chances are Marlon Morrison wasn't doing any work on them anyway, Frank considered. He thought better of saying that as well.

Maravich had been spending the time trying to hunt down anyone else at the lodge who might have encountered the mysterious Barry Fields. Frank located the deputy in the lobby, talking and vigorously taking notes. Marge was behind the counter with the young clerk Frank had encountered the day before. One of the housekeepers was also standing nearby, looking nervous.

Clearly the news of the death of their guest had upset them all, but also aroused their curiosity and sense of excitement.

'Okay, I was able to switch my flight to late Sunday. Now as long as I can extend my stay here, I'm available all weekend.'

Marge forced a brave smile. 'It should be no problem, Mr. Vandegraf. Your room is still available for . . . how long, until Sunday, you say?'

'Yes, thank you, that would be great.'

She reached under the counter and pulled out a new registration form and a pen.

'Goodness, this is just horrible. That poor man. How could such a thing have happened?'

'That's what we'll find out, Marge,' Maravich said, closing his notebook. 'Thank you all for your help.'

He turned to shake hands with Frank. 'You available a little later today, Detective? Maybe a couple hours, so I can gather my facts together and prepare the Sheriff for you?' He made a wry grin. Frank surmised that the sheriff was not going to be as happy about his involvement as Maravich seemed to be.

'Sure. I'll give you a call before I come by.'

'See you then.'

Back in his room, Frank tried calling Francis once again. He got his voice mail again. Apparently the Padre's counseling services were being taken good advantage of.

'Francis, it's Frank. My plans have changed a bit and I'll be here until Sunday. I'd still love to have dinner with you tonight, and maybe spend a little time with you Saturday as well. Give me a call back when you get this.'

Frank had to wonder why he was going to such lengths to be friendly to Francis, a man he had never met before yesterday and who had married his ex-wife. He decided there was something there he needed to work out over time. Guilt, maybe? Regret? He had never blamed Muriel for ending their marriage. When all was said and done, he was a lousy husband. He knew he was prone to distraction and self-absorption, perhaps not always being 'emotionally available,' as the TV shrinks liked to say. Being a cop, especially one 'also married to his job,' as she had put it often, just compounded it. He had always wished her well. He was sure he was genuinely happy to discover that she had been happy here in Easton with Francis. But for whatever reason, he felt some imperative to be nice to Francis. And right now the man sure seemed to need it. He had looked terrible this morning at the service and the burial. In any case it felt like the right way to go.

It didn't take long for Francis to return his call. 'Frank, I need to take care of a few more things but I'd love to meet up for dinner. How about around seven, that work for you?'

That would give him a couple of hours

to spend at the Sheriff's. 'That'd be fine. Where's a good place to meet?'

'Why don't you come over here? I'm not a great chef but I can thaw out a couple of steaks and barbecue them up, add some trimmings and stuff.'

'Are you sure that's okay? Do you really feel up to it? And, well . . . not gonna feel a little strange, having me in your home right now?'

'Frank, I think I'd welcome that. I could use having something to do to keep me busy today. You and I can talk about Muriel and fill each other in. I think we're both okay with that, aren't we?'

'I sure am. If you're positive?'

'Positive.'

'Seven then. Can I bring a bottle of wine? I'm not a big drinker, but maybe this calls for it.'

'Works for me. See you then.'

He returned to the gift shop and found a reasonable-looking bottle of red wine. Marge Palmer was once again behind the counter.

'What a couple of days,' she remarked as she rang up his purchase.

'Tell me about it. Is it always this exciting around here?'

'My gosh, no! I've never seen a week like this one! First Muriel's crazy accident, then Ralph's horrible accident, and now that strange man getting shot. Do you remember much about him?'

Frank cast his eyes around the shop and replayed the short events of the previous day. 'As I told the Deputy, we must have exchanged a half dozen words with each other. I asked him about the cigars he was buying. That was about it. Then I heard your exchange with him here at the counter while he was paying for the stuff he bought.' He recreated the scene of the counter in his mind. Cigars. Shaving cream. Mouthwash. 'He asked you for a bottle of bourbon, didn't he?'

'Why, that's right. A fifth of Rebel Jim. We only carry a couple of brands, so I remember that.'

'He joked about getting ID checked for that.'

'Yes, he used an odd word. 'Proofed', did he say?'

'People say that on the East Coast a lot.

Kids say that. Might be he was from there.'

He bought cigars. Only two. Was that worth noting?

Frank thought about the eyeglasses. Heavy, dark-rimmed. In his mind's eye he tried to conjure up the moment again. What was it . . .

The guy's eyes. The glasses didn't distort them. They were a pretty mild prescription.

Or they were just glass. Fakes. Props.

'Did you talk to him much while he was here at the inn?' Frank asked her.

'No, we spoke briefly when he checked in, the usual stuff. He wasn't into small talk. He wasn't rude or anything, just . . . reticent.'

He bought shaving cream. He knew he was going to shave off his goatee.

He bought mouthwash.

Well . . . okay, not everything had to be meaningful, Frank decided. Maybe for after the bourbon.

'When did he check in?'

'Let's see, you arrived here yesterday, that was Thursday. He checked in

Wednesday night.'

'Did he have a reservation?'

'No. We had plenty of vacancies. He said he didn't need anything fancy, just a simple single.'

'Forgive me, I'm just curious, if you don't mind telling me any of this. Did he happen to mention why he was staying here in Easton for a couple of nights?'

'Oh sure. I guess he was one of the people who had started up an Internet retail site of some kind down in Florida. They were starting to grow and he was scouting out possible locations, I guess where they could set up warehouses, distribution outlets. He said they wanted to find centrally located places where there was a lot of land available at a reasonable price. I gathered he was going to use this as a base of operations and drive around all day yesterday. He even left me a business card. I gave it to the Deputy.'

'And I assume he showed you, what, a driver's license?'

'Yes, he was from Ocala, Florida.'

'And he paid with a credit card, right?'

'Yes, that's right.'

'And he checked out really early.'

'Yes. I wasn't on the desk. It was a couple of hours after midnight. Julius was on duty. Mr. Fields came in, said he got an urgent business call and had to leave, and settled his bill.'

'And I assume Deputy Maravich asked you all that,' Frank smiled. 'I'm not trying to play policeman here or anything. As I said, just curious, like you are. Strange guy, you're right.'

'He apparently made another joke too. Julius said he made a joke about being the company's go-to guy and having to put out some more fires.'

3

Back in his room he decided enough time had passed and he called Maravich, who told him to give him another half hour and then he could come by the station at his convenience. Frank was there in thirty-five minutes.

He was escorted to a small but comfortable conference room. He couldn't help but compare its well-kept cleanliness to the bare-bones-functional rooms of his own unit back home. Maravich sat at a table with the stocky uniformed man Frank had seen earlier. The man rose and extended his hand. 'You must be Detective Vandegraf, right?'

'Frank Vandegraf. You can call me Frank.'

'Sheriff Rick Casullo, Frank.' His bushy mustache and matching eyebrows were salt and pepper toned. The man seemed friendly enough but reserved.

'Lee's filled me in on who you are and

why you are in town. My deepest condolences on your loss. Muriel Lansdowne was a terrific lady.'

Frank nodded acknowledgment.

'Now. Having said that, I appreciate your coming in to confer with us like this, but I'd be less than honest if I didn't tell you up front I do not share my deputy's enthusiasm for it. If it weren't for the fact that Lee Maravich is one hell of a lawman who commands my personal respect as much as any man on this force, I would have in fact overruled his invitation to you, hands down. Nothing personal, I hope you can understand where this is coming from.'

There was an awkward moment of silence among the three. Maravich, sitting back with arms crossed and eyebrows raised, glanced back and forth between the two men to see what would ensue.

Frank rubbed the back of his neck with his hand and sighed. 'No, I understand, Sheriff. I do not take it personally. Earlier today I told Deputy Maravich that in my own department, we do not appreciate carpetbaggers. I don't think any cop anywhere does. But that's not why I'm here. I

73

want to make it clear, I didn't come here to intrude on your investigation or to step into it in any way. I came forth as a witness who spoke with your victim, and to provide background information that may hopefully be of value to your department's investigations. Nothing else. Promise.'

Casullo chewed on that for a long moment — almost literally, it seemed to Frank, as his jaw moved under that walrus mustache.

Finally he gave a terse nod and directed a piercing stare at his visitor. 'All right. I hope that what you've got to offer helps us. I'll leave you two to talk.' He patted Maravich on the shoulder. 'Got a situation that needs my attention. Lee will bring me up to speed later.' He nodded again, shook Frank's hand once again, and left the cubicle.

Maravich gestured for Frank to have a seat and reached for a ceramic mug on the table next to his notepad. 'I'm getting a refill on my coffee. Can I bring you one?'

'Sure.'

Maravich rose. 'Black okay?'

'Black's great,' said Frank.

As he was handed the mug, Frank asked, 'How's the investigation going?'

'Lots more has become known already. Our guy was shot in the head with a twenty-two.'

'A twenty-two, you say?'

Maravich nodded. 'It did the job. Looks like it was a rifle. There are two overpasses along that stretch of the road, a couple hundred feet or so apart. It looks as if the shooter was on or near one overpass and plugged him as he went by. Hit him in the side of the head near the neck. He lost control of the car, must have been doing a good clip, because his momentum carried him pretty forcefully into the piling of the second overpass. The coroner's preliminary report indicates he probably was dead right then.'

'Sounds like a pretty good shot,' Frank mused. 'Car going by at, what, fifty or sixty maybe?'

'That sounds about right.'

'One shot, right?'

'Right. Only one bullet in the victim.'

'So the shooter was lying in wait for him, and must have known he was coming.'

'Sure seems that way. But maybe he wasn't as good as all that. There was only one bullet in the victim, but so far two more bullets have been found near the first overpass. One lodged in a tree by the side of the road.'

Frank digested that. 'Could there have been more than one shooter? Did the bullets all seem to come from the same source?'

'Not totally out of the question. We're still working on the ballistics and such, but so far it's consistent with one shooter only. There were some footprints and what looked like a knee print on the embankment alongside the first overpass. Our guys are still out there going over the site.'

'What's that stretch of road like along there?'

'It feeds into the Interstate about ten or fifteen miles further down the road. Well-traveled during the day, but fairly desolate. Farms, road stands, a gas station or two. No lights, just reflectors along the roadside. A divided county road crosses it and it used to be a grade crossing. After a number of accidents the state finally built overpasses about ten years back.'

'So . . . dark, desolate. A perfect place for an ambush. IF you knew your man was going to be coming through there in the dead of the night.'

Maravich nodded. 'I would say so.'

'I'm curious. If I may ask, what else did you find in his car?'

'Not much. The only thing in the glove compartment was his rental agreement. He picked up the car at the airport Wednesday evening and had an open-end return with an estimation of four days. The return location said New York City.'

'So he was planning on driving across country, it would seem. Was he carrying a weapon?'

'Nope. No gun. He had a multi-tool knife, like a Swiss Army knife kind of thing, in his bag. You know, with blades, screwdrivers, picks . . . '

Frank nodded. 'Sure. Everything imaginable. Scalpel, pitchfork, microwave oven, shortwave radio . . . '

Maravich blinked, then laughed.

'He was traveling light. Small bag. He had only a couple changes of clothes, socks, underwear, all that stuff. A few hygiene articles like a toothbrush. Looked as if he jammed it all in pretty quickly. There was also a small package of business cards, the same kind he gave to Marge at the lodge.'

'Phone?'

'Yeah. One of those month to month cell phones. Like he had picked it up in a hurry somewhere.'

'How about the glasses? Did he have them?'

'As a matter of fact, yes. They were under the seat of the car.'

'Have you had a chance to inspect them? I have a hunch they were props, just clear glass.'

Maravich said they had not done so yet. Frank recounted his recollections of the man's appearance. Maravich began to jot notes down on his legal pad.

'So let's go over this in as much detail as you can, Frank. Why exactly did you have suspicions about this Barry Fields?'

Frank recounted their brief conversation over the cigars. He mentioned the joke he had made about being 'proofed.'

'Okay, so that led you to believe he was

from somewhere on the east coast. But his license did say he was from Florida. And his business cards were from a Florida company.'

'He just struck me as more northeastern seaboard, New York or New England. Not that there aren't a lot of transplants to Florida. But my definite impression was he was at least originally from further north than Florida.'

Maravich asked more questions, prompting Frank to fill in all the details he could remember. The deputy took copious notes, stopping him to clarify points, ask questions and direct the topic along some related avenue. Frank found himself impressed with the man's careful thoroughness. He was beginning to suspect that he would have been a good cop no matter where he lived, someone who would have been a valuable asset in Frank's own Personal Crimes unit.

'Now tell me some more about this Artie Burns guy you think is one and the same person as Barry Fields.'

Frank nodded. 'I can't be sure that was his real name either. His ID was in that name. He said he was an insurance sales-man from Waukegan. He was allegedly passing through town to do a check-in on some contacts. Before we could press him for corroboration of those contacts, his attorney had shown up and was shutting down our interrogation.'

'And from the git-go you weren't buying it. Why did you pick up on him to begin with?'

'Let me back up and tell you about the case we were investigating. It was a guy named Lon Shumer. A real piece of work. We were pretty sure he had his hand in all sorts of things, drugs, numbers, prostitu-tion, you name it. His public face was that he owned a couple of large construction firms and some other ancillary enter-prises. He was smart, I'll give him that. He was a skillful money launderer and he had, like, a battalion of sharp lawyers. We had been after him for years, waiting for him or one of his people to slip up, make some mistake. Someone always does.'

Maravich nodded. 'We don't like to make mistakes, but we get to make a few and we're still in the game. Lawbreakers only get to make one.'

'Exactly. That's one of the few advantages we have on our side. So it was a waiting game on our part. Word came in that Shumer was involved in some kind of labor dispute and that it was getting tense. Worse for him, as it turns out, there were some feelers coming through to us from intermediaries that he might be willing to make some kind of deal.'

'A deal with the police you mean?'

'Yeah. Nothing specific had been established but a couple people from the District Attorney's office came around, floating ideas with us and some of the other units, figuring out what kinds of things might be on the table. They didn't mention Shumer by name but, from the questions they were asking, it was pretty clear to us he was one of the guys they had in mind. We didn't like the idea of him getting any kind of a deal and skating on anything, but it wasn't going to be our call.'

Maravich nodded again. He had stopped writing, caught up in the story Frank was recounting.

'Then late one evening, Shumer took a

dive off a building his company was putting up. The crew coming in early the next morning found him in the debris. There didn't seem to be any witnesses but we located a couple of associates who said they had been drinking with Lon the night before and he had started complaining about the cutbacks and shoddy work that was being done on his building and how he was going to start kicking some butts.'

'And next thing you know, he somehow finds his way up on his building and tumbles off.'

'There you go. Nothing at all suspicious about that, right?'

Maravich smiled grimly, eyebrows raised, and shook his head.

'So how did this Burns character fit into this scenario? How did you come to suspect him?'

'It was part footwork and part dumb luck. As I said, we smelled a rat. His 'friends' who were telling us about the drinking, they were a little sketchy to us too. We were checking security cameras around the site for that night and found a photo of the guy making a transaction at a nearby ATM. We lucked out on a canvas of nearby hotels. He was staying at a hotel about six blocks away. And he was checking out when we got there.'

'Seems like if he was the fixer you thought, he would have been long gone. What was this, a day or two later?'

'Almost twenty-four hours later. Another piece of luck on our part, a major storm somewhere in the Midwest. His flight had been cancelled. He couldn't re-book until the weather cleared, and those flights were stacked up.'

'Where was he flying to? You said he claimed to be from Waukegan, that's near Chicago.'

'His flight was to Chicago, but here's the thing, we found out he also had a connector on to Boston.'

'Hmm. So you picked this guy up and brought him in for questioning?'

'Right. That's when we got the story. His ID said he was Arthur Burns. He said he went by Artie. He dragged his feet with us, refused to answer many questions but did say he said he was an insurance salesman making cold calls . . . and then the mouthpiece walked through the door.'

'You couldn't hold him.'

Frank shook his head. 'We didn't have enough. He and his major-league lawyer walked out the door, Mr. Burns got in a cab and got on his plane, I assume, and that was the last we ever saw of him.'

'Did you follow up on the information you did have?'

'Sure. Guess what. We couldn't find any trace of an insurance man named Artie Burns from Waukegan or anywhere else. We turned up a few guys with the name but they didn't match.'

'What about the lawyer who sprung him?'

'He was an out of town guy too, up from the Los Angeles area. A partner in a firm that we later figured had some dubious connections of its own with murky figures. We tried to contact him, but he refused to talk with us about the event. Simply said it was a closed deal, we had picked up an innocent man; that was that. Wouldn't divulge how he had been connected with or contacted by our suspect.

In the end Artie Burns was just dust in the wind.'

'One that got away. You were sure you had the right guy.'

'We had the sense he was good for it. You know the feeling. Nothing else we pursued ever panned out in any way near as right. We only got more sure of it as time went by. We picked up rumors that Lon had run afoul of some organization types back East in New England and that they had taken some steps when they got worried about his possibly turning snitch.'

'That's quite a story, Detective.'

'Call me Frank. I'm just a citizen here in your territory.'

'So what is it about this guy that makes you so sure Artie Burns could have been Barry Fields? You said the eyes?'

Frank nodded. 'I was only in the room with him for half an hour at best, probably less. He couldn't have said more than fifty, sixty words to us. But he had that snake gaze I mentioned to you before. Icy cold intelligence. I could believe he was a stone killer. He just felt capable of it.'

'But otherwise, you said he looked

different from this guy Barry Fields?'

'Very different. He had that thick mustache but otherwise he was clean-shaven. As I recall, his hair was fuller and darker. He had an ordinary dark brown suit, the kind of thing you'd expect an insurance salesman to wear. No glasses.'

'Height and weight about right?'

'It's been a while, but yeah, I'd say so. I stood alongside Burns and I stood alongside Fields and it was the same angle, more or less.'

'So, assuming this guy Burns was your out of town killer and he had arranged the accident that killed Shumer, any luck tracing down the alias, if it had been used before?'

'Zero on that. The guy was experienced. We guessed he assumed a new identity every time he went out, altered his appearance in simple ways, obtained documentation, then got rid of it all upon his exit. Our one lead was that he likely had been recruited by the Boston mob. We did some research into alleged activities by the guy we were told had it in for Lon Shumer. We talked to law enforcement in that area, even Feds.

We found three other suspicious deaths over a five-year period. Nothing that could be pinned on anyone but there were things that stood out in those cases.'

'Such as?'

'They were all apparent accidents. Nobody had been shot, stabbed, strangled, beaten to death. One was a boating accident, a guy who was said to be an excellent swimmer. One was a guy whose car stalled on a railroad track in front of an oncoming train. One was an electrocution in the home with nobody else around.'

'And they all gave cause for suspicion, you say. Interesting.'

'All three could be traced back to the Boston mob guy, maybe a little tenuously but the connection was always there. They happened in different cities but all three times local law enforcement were hesitant to close the door on the deaths.'

'So you began to suspect that this Artie Burns guy was behind these accidents. He was, like you said, a professional fixer.'

'Nothing anybody could prove. Cops in different places sharing instincts. But I'm not a fan of the concept of coincidence.'

'Which leads me to the next question. Assuming Barry Fields is the same guy, he could only be in Easton on an assignment.' Maravich left the remainder of the thought hanging in the air for a long moment.

'And lo and behold,' Frank finally said, 'you have this remarkable accidental death only the night before.'

Maravich crossed his hands over his chest, took a deep breath and sighed heavily. 'Lord help us. Sheriff Casullo is not ready to believe Ralph Watkins was anything but an accident.'

'Tell me a little bit about it, if you can? What exactly do they think happened?'

'Ralph closes his station every evening around dinner time. Maybe five or six. He was a bit of a hermit, kept to himself mostly, turned up now and then at the diner or the bar or at a store or market, but usually just kept to himself. He lived a ways down the road from the station in an old farmhouse. Anyway, the prevailing wisdom is that he decided to have himself a few nips before going home and possibly got too involved in that undertaking.

From the evidence, it looks as if he sat himself down out front of his station too near the pumps and lit himself up a cigar. There was a leak or a spill from the pump and . . . *boom!* Explosion that could be heard a block away. Big fire. By the time the fire department got to him, he was burned almost beyond recognition.'

'So if he had been assaulted in any way, let's say for the sake of argument, there would have been no evidence left on his body since it was burned up.'

'For the sake of argument, correct. If there were reason to suspect said assault, of course.'

'No question it was Ralph, though, right?'

'Dental records confirmed it. One thing Ralph did do was visit the doc and the dentist regularly.'

'How are they so sure he was drunk and was smoking? I told you, I had a brief conversation with him earlier that same day and he told me he had sworn off both.'

'They actually found remnants of the cigar and pieces of the bottle. It was pretty clear.'

Frank covered his eyes with his hand and thought for a moment. Still holding that position, he asked, 'Any idea what kind of cigar and what kind of booze?'

Maravich pulled a manila folder out from under his notepad and pulled out some papers, leafing through them. 'Nobody's gone to the trouble of identifying the remnants of the cigar. The bottle was amber-colored and square. Black label.'

'Ever see a bottle of Rebel Jim bourbon?'

'Probably. Can't quite picture it. Wait a second.' Maravich hit Frank's wavelength all at once. His eyes widened.

'It's a square, amber-tinted bottle with a narrow neck about three inches long. Black label. That's what Barry Fields was buying at the gift shop. Along with a couple of cigars.'

Maravich picked up a phone and asked the operator for a number.

'Marge, hi, it's Lee over at the Sheriff's. I asked you not to disturb Mr. Fields' room yet . . . great, nobody's been in there? Nothing's been cleaned or removed? That's real good. I'm going to be over in a little while, okay? Do me another favor, don't empty any of the garbage bins around the lodge until I get a chance to look things over? Thanks.'

The deputy hung up and looked at Frank. 'I'm hoping to be wrong, but I'm thinking we are not going to find a whiskey bottle or any remains of a cigar in Mr. Fields' room. Or disposed of anywhere around the lodge.'

'So you're starting to think I might not be crazy about Ralph Watkins, then,' Frank said.

'Why would some gangster type come out here to kill old Ralph?' Maravich asked. 'And then why would he get killed himself? This is still crazy. Maybe it all is just a bunch of strange coincidences.'

'As I said,' Frank replied, 'in my experience there is no such thing. Maybe your experience has been different.'

The deputy chewed on that for a bit and began to shake his head slowly back and forth. 'No, sir. It has not. Things generally happen for a reason, once all the facts are in.'

'Once all the facts are in,' Frank said,

nodding. 'What do you really know about Ralph Watkins, anyway?'

'Not much. He moved here maybe two, three years ago. Bought that old farmhouse and service station. He's a good mechanic. Well, he was a good mechanic.'

'Did he ever tell anyone where he came from, why he moved here? I mean no offense to this lovely town, but this is kind of off the beaten path.'

'He said he came here to forget. That in essence is what he's told anyone nosing into his affairs. Nobody seems to have gotten many details but he said he lost his family in a terrible tragedy and came here to forget. He's always been a nice enough sort, just kept himself at arm's length from everybody who tried to get close.'

'Apparently my ex-wife was one of those people trying to make a reclamation project out of him.'

'Muriel was fond of lost puppies and kittens, even the human sort that is true. But you knew that.'

'Oh yeah. That was her all right. And when the kindness wasn't in gear, the curiosity was. I can see her trying to get the goods on Ralph Watkins. But she apparently didn't succeed either, so the guy was a regular clam, it would seem.'

'Yes he was.'

'Whatever was in his past, he seems to have reason to keep it bottled up. In a manner of speaking.'

'And you say he told you he wasn't drinking anymore.'

'Or smoking.'

'I'll do some asking around, but I don't know that anyone has talked about seeing him at the roadhouse tavern of late.'

'Father McNulty, over at the church, told me much the same thing. He was sure that Ralph wasn't drinking anymore also. This whole thing bothered him as well.'

'I'll make a point to go speak with the Padre tonight after I go back to the Sportsman.'

'One other thing. You said there were some other people asking questions about Ralph's death?'

'Oh yeah. They really put a bug up Rick Casullo's you-know-where. They're driving him crazy. They also got a team in a van that sealed off the service station today, just came in and took over. They even sent our deputies away, and they were not nice about it. That's a way to get on his bad side for sure.'

'Would they be the man and woman in the dark suits I saw with the Sheriff earlier?'

'The same.'

'They look like FBI to me. I don't suppose . . . '

'Actually,' Maravich said, 'they're Federal Marshals.'

'Marshals! Really!'

'Rick told me he's got no idea why they're here or what they want, but he seems a little tentative about that and I wonder. They seem to agree with him that the death was accidental. But they're asking around, an awful lot of questions. You'll likely see them, they must be staying at the Sportsman too.'

'Marshals. I'm thinking what you find Federal Marshals doing.'

'Don't see them much around here. They transport prisoners, don't they? And run down fugitives.'

'Something else they do, Deputy.'

'Uh huh, and that would be?'

'They run the Federal Witness Protection Program.'

4

'I'm just gonna clear off the dishes here quick. Why don't you go sit in the living room? I'll be right in.'

'Sure I can't give you a hand with those, Francis?'

'Naw, I'm just gonna pile 'em up in the kitchen and throw 'em in the dishwasher later. Then I'm gonna visit the little boy's room for a moment and then make myself an after-dinner drink. Can I bring you one?'

'No, thanks,' Frank said, rising from the table. Half a bottle of wine was more than he usually drank. Francis had also had a couple of stiff shots before dinner. Frank had to give him some slack on that. This had not been a good day for him and he seemed to be carrying its full weight. 'Hey, great steaks.'

That brought a smile. 'Hadn't used the barbecue in a while. Guess I haven't lost my touch.'

'Not by my lights.' Frank wandered into the living room and aimed himself at a comfortable-looking stuffed chair.

'Be right back. Make yourself at home.'

Frank looked around the room and spotted what looked like a school yearbook on a nearby coffee table. He picked it up and sat down in the chair. It was every bit as comfortable as it had looked to be. The yearbook turned out to be from Lafferty College in Massachusetts from some years back. On a hunch he leafed through the section on seniors and found a picture of one 'Frank Lansdowne,' a younger and callower version of his host. It made him smile. He browsed through more of the section at a series of unfamiliar names and faces.

'I see you found my old Lafferty yearbook.'

'Yeah, you had it out on the table. Amazing to think how young we all were once, isn't it?'

Francis sat down on the sofa across from Frank and placed a tall glass on the table. It was full of amber liquid and ice cubes. 'Yeah. I was reminiscing the other day and pulled it out.'

Frank closed the book and put it on the table in front of him. 'So you went to school on the East Coast. Lafferty's a good school.'

Francis nodded. 'I was lucky to get in. Even got some financial aid.'

'What did you major in?'

'Business. I planned to move to someplace like New York or Boston and become a world beater.'

'That plan would seem to have changed.'

'Right after school I got an entry-level job in a firm in Connecticut, but then my dad got sick. He ran a hardware and automotive supply business. I decided to come back home and help rescue the two stores. After he passed away, I stayed on. I still run them today.'

'And it was after that that you met Muriel here.'

'Well, we knew each other in high school, though we were a couple of years apart. When she moved back here, she came to work for the stores, doing our book-keeping . . . and we got re-acquainted.'

Frank nodded with a smile. 'And the rest is history.'

'Guess so.'

'Did she continue to work for you after that?'

'Naw. That was kind of something to tread water for her. She really wanted to teach. She taught middle school for a while, ran the school library.'

'She went back to teaching. That's interesting. What was her subject?'

'English, social studies . . . kinda fits in with her interests and all.'

'Definitely. That's what she was doing when we were married, teaching junior high, or middle school, whatever they call it now. Then the system started to grind her down. In some ways, being in the public school system in a big city is similar to what I do. A lot of banging your head against a wall. But Muriel had a lot more idealism than I do, I guess, and got tired of that constant Quixotic struggle with the bureaucracy. She decided to give it up and go back to school. I guess she picked up accounting along the way.' In fact Muriel had still been in school when they split up. He realized he hadn't even known what courses she took. The memories made him uncomfortable. He found himself gazing around the room. 'This was her family's house?'

'Uh-huh. When her folks passed away, she inherited it. It made sense for us to move in here. Much nicer and roomier than my old place.'

'It looks as if you two were very happy together. That's a good thing.'

'We were, Frank. We really were.'

'She deserved to be happy. I'm afraid I wasn't a very good husband on that score.'

'For what it's worth, I never — well, let's say almost never — heard complaints from Muriel. What she did say about you was almost entirely good.'

'I keep hearing that, but . . . really?'

'If she spoke about your marriage at all, she mostly would say it hadn't been meant to go on, and she'd leave it at that.'

Frank leaned forward and rested his elbows on his thighs. He sat pensive for some time, staring at the carpet, and finally spoke.

'You probably know she came out West to go to school. After she graduated was when she met me. I had just been promoted to Detective. I guess she thought I seemed . . . dashing or exciting or something.'

'She told me about meeting you. Some kind of break-in at her apartment.'

'Right. A burglary. I was just taking facts, investigating. A couple of months later we caught the guy. He was a druggie hitting the neighborhood apartments. I went back to fill her in and asked her out for coffee.'

'I suspect that wasn't something you did with every single burglary victim.'

Frank just raised his eyebrows and smiled a little.

'And the rest is history,' Francis said, returning a smile of his own.

'There you go.'

'Muriel had this big interest in crime and cops and mysteries and the whole thing. She loved mystery stories and crime fiction.'

'Yes she did. I think it came as a disappointment to her just how prosaic the real thing is. How time-consuming and frustrating.'

'She said she got you into watching mysteries on TV and reading them, because you liked to deconstruct them and tell her exactly how inaccurate they were.'

Frank shook his head and sighed loudly. 'That was me. You know, I still do that. She got me hooked on those damned things. Just so I can go, 'Ah-*hah*! Got *that* wrong too!' Kind of crazy.' He looked up at Francis. 'She must have told you about all the nights I wasn't there. Even when I was home. Too much in my head.'

'Yeah. A little bit. But I think she understood, Frank. That was your life. She always said you cared. You cared about the victims. About the job. About doing the right thing. And she always said that was hard for you.'

'It's hard for all of us who do what I do. You see all kinds of things . . . the depths people can sink to. You honestly do want to make a difference. There are always obstacles and roadblocks. As I said, the best it can be is really frustrating. At worst it's straight out dehumanizing. There's that temptation to feel sorry for yourself, to start to think that nobody understands. But what was harder for me to realize was, that wasn't the real issue. The real issue was that whether or not she understood, I couldn't be available for her. I couldn't be there.' He looked down again. 'Not even when I *was* there. Physically, I mean. It began to dawn on me that maybe I was incapable of being there for anybody else. In the end, it was clear-cut what we had to do.'

'Did she ever tell you about me? I mean, after she moved back here and all.'

'We didn't communicate much after she returned to Easton. She sent me a couple of letters, we had maybe a couple of phone calls. In what, nine or ten years?'

'We would have been married eight years this August. So yeah, that would be about when she moved back here.'

'Funny, one of the few things I remember her telling me was that you liked cigars. That, and that you owned a hardware store.'

'Two stores, actually. They're next door to one another along Main Street. Yes, our main drag is actually called Main Street. And there's an Elm Street and a Maple Street too. Like something out of a story, huh?'

'In fact there's a West Elm and an East Elm,' Frank said, remembering the address of the Theodore Rollins Funeral Home.

'On either side of Main. Also a West and East Maple. And Oak. And Sycamore. The founding fathers were optimistic.'

They both laughed a little.

'Anyway, the stores are called Lands Hardware and Lands Automotive. My dad figured shortening the name gave it a better recognition factor.'

'So when did you stop being Frank and become Francis?'

'When I left college. I figured it gave me more, I don't know, gravitas or something. My mother used to call me Francis. When I went to college, I wanted to be different so I told people I was Frank. I hung out with a bunch of frat boys in school and when that was over, I figured it was time to get more serious. Something like that. I haven't gone by Frank in many years.'

'Just as well,' said Frank. 'It might have been confusing this week, between us both.'

'True. Confusing enough as it was.'

'So, all those guys you partied with in college, how did they all turn out?'

'Some of them went back to take over their family businesses too. But they weren't hardware stores in the Midwest, they were, like, law firms and ad agencies. There were even a couple of guys from mob families, and heaven knows what they wound up doing.'

'A number of those kinds of guys would send their kids to school to get them out of the business, get them into something legitimate.'

'Could be. I never kept in touch with anyone from those years. Once I got back here I burned my bridges. In fact I almost never left town again. There was our honeymoon, when Muriel and I went to the Bahamas. That was about it. Aside from that, I've been here in Easton and never felt the need to go anywhere else.'

After a short silence, Frank changed the subject.

'I'm just curious. Did Ralph Watkins ever buy automotive parts or stuff like that from you?'

'Oh, sure. All the time.'

'Did you guys talk much?'

Francis shrugged.

'Probably as much as anybody did with Ralph. He was friendly enough but not much on talking.'

'Did he say much about his past, his family, anything?'

'Not really. He once said he came here to forget. Never anything more specific than that. I gathered that something traumatic happened to him. Maybe he lost his family in an accident or something, or maybe there was a really harsh divorce. There was just him, living in that house and running that gas station.'

'I would think sooner or later a man living all alone like that would find the need for someone to talk to, you know?'

'Well, Ralph did drink a bit, at least when he first came out here. He hung out at the local watering hole some evenings.

On occasion I'd stop by there after a particularly bad day at the store, or like that, and I'd sometimes see him there. Seemed as if he mostly watched whatever sports were on and talked inconsequential stuff with the guys at the bar. If he had a confidant or a close friend, I sure never knew about it.'

'Or a girlfriend or something, you know?'

Francis took another gulp from his drink and raised his eyebrows. 'I know. You'd think.'

'It seems that Muriel thought along similar lines, huh? She wanted to fix him up with someone?'

'Yeah. She tried to make a reclamation case out of old Ralph. She talked about inviting him to groups she was involved with, and so forth. He wasn't having any part of it.'

'Did she ever try to introduce him to anyone specific? I could see Muriel doing that, you know?'

Francis laughed.

'Yeah, yeah. For sure. No, she talked about it, tried bouncing various ideas off of me. 'What about so-and-so, think they'd get along?' I never encouraged her. My feeling was always that Ralph wanted to be alone, needed to work out whatever it was he needed to work out, and we should respect that. She never acted on any of that, just talked it over with me and her other friends.'

'Sounds like she learned a bit about Ralph's background after all. Like that TV character we were talking about, the detective's wife.'

'Ha! Yeah. I do think she tried different ploys to get him to drop some little bits of information to her, but I doubt she ever succeeded. Ralph was elusive. Downright slippery when he wanted to be. And, when you come down to it, people in this town respect privacy. I don't know if you've ever lived in a really small rural town like Easton?'

'Nope. I grew up in the city. Urban all my life.'

'There's this strange and charming dichotomy. On the one hand, we're a small village and everybody knows everybody else and everybody has this sense of protectiveness and togetherness. We're like a family. Or a tribe. It's hard to do anything without everyone else knowing about it right away. But then on the other hand, there's a sense of respecting limits. There's a line past which you don't ever go. Someone else's business is theirs and theirs alone. That's a sort of family thing as well. You don't find either one observed quite so strictly in a large city.'

Frank nodded. 'So a guy like Ralph couldn't quite hide, but he could be sort of anonymous in plain sight.'

'Something like that, yeah.'

★   ★   ★

Francis had unearthed a box of photos and they looked through them, passing them back and forth. Francis told stories and gave background and seemed to lighten his own mood considerably. It was surprisingly not very awkward for Frank at all. The evening turned out to be a comfortable one. Finally Frank looked at his watch and began to make his goodbyes, thanking Francis for dinner and the company.

'Frank, something I need to tell you,'

Francis said as they rose.

'What's that?'

'Clearly there's something that's been on your mind about you and Muriel. I don't know exactly what it might be, but believe me, you should put it to rest. You did okay by her, Frank. You couldn't give her what you didn't have to give. You did the best you could. Muriel understood that.' He looked Frank straight in the eye and extended his hand.

'Thanks, Francis.' They shook hands and he turned to leave.

* * *

When Frank finally pulled into the parking lot of the Sportsman, he saw several people congregating around a dark sedan and a van parked nearby. The man and woman he had seen earlier at the Sheriff's station were among them, now in dark windbreakers rather than suits. Large yellow letters on the back proclaimed U. S. MARSHAL in bold. They all looked as if it had been a long day.

The woman spotted Frank as he got

out of his car, made a comment to her partner, and they approached him. They were both dark-haired and serious.

The woman spoke when they were a few feet away. 'Excuse me, you're Detective Vandegraf, I believe?'

'Around here, I'm just plain Frank Vandegraf, but yes.'

She produced a folding case with ID and a badge. 'I'm Deputy United States Marshal Candace Maldonado. This is Deputy United States Marshal Franco Bartolli. Could we have a moment of your time?'

Frank sighed. It had been a long day and all he really wanted was some sleep.

'Sure.'

'We understand you've been asking about last night's incident involving the nearby service station fire and death of the owner.'

'I've talked about it with a couple of people, yes.'

'May I ask your interest in the incident?' Maldonado, Frank noted, appeared quite at home with the scowl that seemed set on her face. Bartolli maintained a similar grimace and said nothing.

'Driving in yesterday, I stopped at the station and had a very brief conversation with the owner, Ralph Watkins. In the course of that conversation he happened to mention that he had stopped drinking and smoking. Subsequently, I heard that his death was attributed to an accident caused by his drinking heavily and carelessly lighting a cigar near his gas pumps. It just struck me as odd, and I happened to mention that to some people I encountered here in Easton.'

'You went to the Sheriff's Department and discussed it with a deputy.'

'I did. As you know, I'm a police detective. I did what I would have wanted someone in my own jurisdiction to do if they thought they had information that might be of interest in the investigation.'

'Have you ever had any other communication with Ralph Watkins at any time?'

'Nope. We exchanged a few sentences when I gassed up. That was it.'

Maldonado eyed him carefully.

'And who else have you shared this observation with?'

'Just one or two people who knew him.'

He left it at that.

Bartolli finally piped up. 'We understand you've also been talking about another individual that you encountered here, who was involved in a separate incident today?'

'You mean Barry Fields. He was a guest here at the lodge and we also exchanged a few words. That was it. I mentioned that as well to the Deputy Sheriff when I was at the station.'

'You seem to be showing a lot of interest in the goings-on around here.'

Frank tried to mask his growing impatience. 'As I said, I simply came forward to offer whatever small information I might have. That's it.'

Maldonado took over once again.

'Detective, can you tell us exactly why you're here?'

Frank returned Maldonado's scowl along with a steady stare for a long moment before replying. 'I came here to bury my ex-wife. But I think you knew that already, didn't you?'

Maldonado waited a beat or two before her own answer. 'My condolences for your loss, sir. May we assume you'll be leaving soon?'

'I actually would have been gone by now, but I moved my flight. I'm departing Sunday.'

'It seems surprising you're staying around that long.'

'It was the soonest they could give me. Believe me, I've got no interest in hanging around here any longer than I need to. I seem to be getting diminishing returns on my stay.' He maintained his own steadfast glare back at the Marshals.

'All right. Your willingness to come forward and contribute what you know is greatly appreciated, Detective. There happens to be an ongoing investigation and we're sure you can appreciate the need for it to be free of any outside interference.'

'Interference has never been my intention,' Frank said. It came out more abrupt than he had planned.

'I'm sure you understand that we're conducting an ongoing *confidential* investigation. There is also quite a bit of which you are, necessarily, *not* aware, and that we need to keep it that way.'

'Of course, Deputy.' He evenly moved his gaze from Maldonado to Bartolli and back again. He considered asking a few more questions, bringing up the subject of witness protection, but definitely thought better of it. He only momentarily considered expounding upon his suspicions about Barry Fields, but quickly dismissed that thought as well. He simply let the silence hang awkwardly.

They all exchanged a few more meaningful looks before Maldonado nodded and said tersely, 'Thank you, sir, I think we understand each other then. Have a good night.'

Neither made an effort to shake Frank's hand. They walked away to join the rest of the Marshals and Frank turned toward his own room.

Suddenly something struck him. Funny how that worked.

You toss something around in your mind, worry it to death, can't grasp some elusive fact or detail. Then you leave it alone. Your brain keeps working on it in the background.

Frank referred to it as 'putting it on the

back burner,' where it would keep roiling until suddenly something fell into place.

He remembered why Ralph Watkins had seemed familiar to him.

He glanced back at Maldonado and Bartolli and their companions as they walked to their own rooms.

He was sure he had it.

5

As tired as he was, his racing brain would not allow him to rest. Frank finally got to sleep but it was fitful. He set an alarm to be up reasonably early Saturday morning. There were things he wanted to do.

After breakfast he found Marge behind the reception counter.

'Don't you ever take a day off?'

She smiled. 'Good morning, Mr. Vandegraf. Oh, I'm just watching out for things until Julius comes in for his week-end shift. When you run the business, things never stop.'

'That's true.'

'So what can I do for you this morning?'

'I was wondering if there's a computer available somewhere, where I can go on the Internet.'

'You know you've got free wi-fi in your room, right?'

'Unfortunately that won't help me since I don't have a laptop with me.' In fact, Frank didn't even own one, but he figured it wasn't worth going into. 'Maybe there's a library nearby, or you've got a computer available?'

'Sure, we have a business center with two Internet ready computers.'

She reached under the counter and brought out a key attached to a small plastic plate.

'Honestly, calling it a 'business center' is kind of ambitious. There's a small conference table, a couple of terminals that type of thing. It's really not very big, but just your luck, it's all yours today.'

'Thank you. I might need it a while.'

'Shouldn't be a problem. It's the room right down the hall on your right.' She scrawled some numbers on a slip of paper and passed it over to him.

'Here's your username and password.'

'Great. And I figure I can find a small notebook in the gift shop, right?'

★ ★ ★

'Well, fancy meeting you here.'

Frank turned around from the monitor and closed the notebook in which he had been feverishly jotting. 'Well, Deputy. Looking for me by any chance?'

Maravich pulled up a chair and sat down. 'Marge told me you'd be back here. I came over to investigate about our friend Mr. Fields some more, but I also wanted to have another chat with you. You know, fill you in on developments, see if you've got any other input that might be of help.'

'I'm assuming this is not at the behest of Sheriff Casullo.'

Maravich raised his eyebrows.

'My behest solely, that's correct.'

'After last night, I have the distinct idea that my 'input' isn't all that welcome around here.'

'Ahh. I gather you met up with the Marshals then? They do seem to be a piece of work, don't they? They've been really giving Rick Casullo a hard time too. Even got somebody from back in D.C. to call him, and more than once. He just wants to see them gone and this whole thing over and done.'

Maravich glanced at the computer screen. 'You don't strike me as a man with a lot of social media going on.'

'Nope. My twentieth birthday is well past, I fear.'

'So I'm thinking you're still doing some research into things we talked about?'

'Back home I have a bit of a reputation among my colleagues as a dinosaur. Not very accomplished in the digital world. I've got an old flip phone and I don't have a laptop. But I figured I'd navigate my way around a few things this morning just to kill some time since I'm a captive audience here until my flight tomorrow. I can do that, find my way around cyberspace with a little blundering and a little luck.'

'And how's that working out?' The deputy smiled.

'I have a colleague back in my squad, Jill Garvey, who's technically very savvy. She's always kidding me about being a Luddite. She'd be proud of me today. I am actually finding things. Sometimes I surprise myself.'

'What kind of things?'

'Just answering a couple questions that were bugging me. What can I tell you, I'm just a cop. I'll be gone and out of your hair pretty soon, and whatever I give you is yours to do with as you please.'

Maravich shook his head and looked weary. 'I don't know that anything is going to be of much use, to be honest with you. I'm finding myself up against what I guess you'd call politics and such. I might be grasping at straws when all is said and done. But I'm happy to take whatever you've got, in any case.'

'I've got a few things we can talk about. But first, Deputy, I have a question for you.'

'Shoot.'

'Is there any possibility that Muriel Lansdowne's death was not an accident?'

Maravich crossed his arms, shook his head and laughed quietly.

'Frank, you really are trying to stir up trouble around here, aren't you?'

'It's just I've never been a big fan of coincidence. I think we talked about that before. In the past few days, you've probably had more deaths than you've seen in quite a while, isn't that true? I mean, *curious* deaths.'

Maravich stared at Frank with a small smile on the corners of his mouth. It seemed he was trying to decide whether to take him seriously or not.

'Frank Vandegraf comes to town and all hell breaks loose.'

'Really. Has the Department given it any consideration at all?'

'That Muriel's death was a homicide, you mean? That's a stretch. A big stretch.' He shook his head again and looked at the ground in thought. 'No. She fell off a ladder. There's nothing that would indicate anything else.'

'It's just a little odd. Francis said he was surprised she would go up on that ladder by herself. What if someone else was there with her?'

'The only person that comes to mind would be Francis himself. Are you suggesting he killed his wife?'

'I don't know what I'm suggesting. There's just something off there.'

'Frank, here we are back at coincidences

again, and I'm still no fan of them, but sometimes things just happen. I just don't see it.'

Maravich directed his gaze back at Frank. 'In fact that's one of the things I came here to tell you about. Damnedest thing.'

'Should we maybe go get a cup of coffee or something and talk? Then we can come back here and maybe I can show you some things.'

'Sounds good to me. The restaurant here has much better coffee than the station, that's a fact.'

$$\star \quad \star \quad \star$$

Maravich thanked the waitress for his mug of steaming coffee and took an appreciative sip. 'So here's the strange thing I was starting to tell you about. I told you we found footprints and what looked like a knee print on the embankment of that first overpass.'

'I remember.'

'We also found shells. Not just one or two. Nine altogether.'

'Twenty-twos?'

'Yes. And what looks like the last remains of a marijuana joint, what the kids call a roach. And an empty potato chip bag and an empty soda can.'

'Hardly sounds like a professional shooter to me.'

'It certainly does not. But there's more.'

Frank took a sip of his own coffee and leaned forward, fascinated by this bizarre new development.

'I think I mentioned that we found two other slugs on the other side of the roadway. One was in a tree, one in another embankment. Our guys found another one lodged in the concrete of the overpass.'

'Okay. And?'

'And then there's this. We got a call yesterday from a lady named Charice Barnes. She lives a couple miles from here and she's a registered nurse, what you call a traveling nurse. Right now she's working at Mercy General Hospital, which is about forty miles down the road. That same road. She has to get up very early for her shift and drives that way.'

'So you're saying she was on the road around the same time as Barry Fields yesterday morning.'

'It seems so, yes. Coroner hasn't established the exact time of death yet but it seems safe that it was around four A.M. Charice was coming through there somewhere around that time.'

'Okay.'

'She told us she heard a loud noise against the side of her car. She was alone in the dark on a deserted stretch of road, so she was scared to stop and investigate. I don't blame her. Her car seemed to be driving okay so she kept going all the way to the hospital. Once she felt safe in the lighted parking lot, she checked out her car. There was a bullet hole in her right rear fender.'

'A bullet hole?'

'That's right. She called us after her shift and we had her bring the car over for us to take a look at. The bullet was there, in the trunk of her car.'

'And it was a twenty-two, I'm guessing.'

Maravich nodded.

'We've got footprints from a hunting boot, a knee print that looks to be from jeans, a soda can we can pull prints off. There's a local family with two teenage kids who are a little bit off, shall we say. We've had trouble with them a few times.'

'You're thinking your hit man got killed by a kid taking pot shots off the embankment in the middle of the night?'

'By the way, we can't be sure that he was a hit man yet. But yes . . . there were complaints about one of the boys doing something similar a month or two ago.'

Frank rubbed the back of his neck. 'So you're saying at this point it's looking like everything's a grand coincidence of weird events.'

'I'm saying only that it's the most consistent with the evidence. We follow the evidence, am I right?'

'I can't argue that. Of course you do. It's just . . . '

'I know. It's strange.'

'I assume you've been talking to the boys in question.'

'A couple deputies went by their home last night. Brought them in. Lem and

Lyle. A little history of trouble with both boys, nothing all that serious. The whole family's a little off. Their father was a vet, came back from overseas with post-traumatic syndrome. But maybe I'm telling tales out of school now.'

'One or both of them own twenty-twos, I'm guessing?'

Maravich nodded.

'Several weapons in that family, including a couple twenty-twos. We have them in custody.'

Frank shook his head. 'A kid sitting near a bridge late at night, shooting at random passing cars and trucks. Could that really be all of it?'

'As soon as we've matched up the slugs and shells to one of the guns, I suspect, yes.'

Frank chewed on that for a while. 'It still doesn't explain what that Barry Fields guy was doing here. Or why he checked out and was leaving in the dead of the night.'

'I have to agree. One possibility is he really was who he said he was, a guy representing that company Irrawaddy, and he was on his way to do some more location scouting. But . . . '

'But?' Frank prompted.

Maravich looked abashed. 'We've tried to find out more about him, to try to contact next of kin and so forth. So far it's a dead end.'

'Is the company real?'

'It would seem. There's a real site, at any rate, but it's just got a place-holder image at the moment, just says 'Coming soon, watch this site!' and some other things to that effect.'

'And let me venture a guess: his card didn't have a telephone number?'

'He had written his cell number on a few of the cards. That was it.'

'Have you checked out his phone? You said it was a burner of some sort.'

'Yep. The number matched. Bought it with prepaid minutes at the airport. The kind you can add more minutes to if you want, with a credit card.'

'That's kind of weird for a sales rep or whatever, wouldn't you say?'

'I think so. But I also know that some of these Internet startups are pretty unorthodox. Slippery folks. I'm sure you've encountered the people I mean, right?'

'Yes,' Frank sighed. 'Yes, I have.'

'Running on hope and promises. Need to come across impressive. They've got no money, but want to make it look as if they do, so they run on the cheap but try to make it all look slick and corporate. It's all hat and no cattle, like some of my relatives down in Texas like to say.'

'I think you're giving this guy a huge benefit of the doubt, Deputy.'

'I'm just trying to stay objective, Frank. But my doubt grows by the minute as we're unable to find any trace of somebody named Barry Fields.'

'And suppose he wasn't who he said he was? Then what are the alternatives?'

'Your suggestion certainly has to stay in play.'

'That he came here to eliminate Ralph Watkins.'

'There are a lot of people not liking that idea, let me tell you. But yes, I have to keep it in mind.'

Frank downed the remainder of his

coffee and picked up the check lying on the table. 'Come on back to the computer with me. I've got some things to show you that you might find interesting.'

* * *

The newspaper was about three and a half years old, and the front page filled the screen. The headline screamed in huge dark type across the top of the page.

TESTIMONY NAILS MOB BOSS

Maravich scanned the article rapidly. 'Pat Fine. I remember reading about him. One of the big shots in the New England organization.'

Frank scrolled down on the page to a photo at the bottom. Its caption read

TESTIMONY OF FINE UNDERLING
LARRY WARNECKE PAINTS DAMNING
EVIDENCE THAT COULD SEAL HIS FATE!

'Take a good look at that photo. Look familiar?'

'It's not a great reproduction. Hard to tell.'

'Right. So then let's go here . . . ' Frank clicked the mouse a few times and toggled over to another web page. This one was a popular online encyclopedia. The entry read RAYMOND LAWRENCE 'LARRY' WARNECKE at the top. The introduction described Warnecke as 'a former associate of the Fine crime family. He is known as the man who helped bring down Pat Fine, the family's boss, by agreeing to become a Federal witness.' The article continued at some length.

'He was a well-connected guy. Pretty high up in the scheme of things, responsible for collections, the kind of guy who might have possession of incriminating records of various sorts. Something happened to his wife and child. They were in a car that drove off a bridge and they were killed. Warnecke apparently concluded someone in the organization was responsible, possibly Fine himself. It almost seems like it became a personal vendetta between those two. He turned state's evidence with a vengeance.'

The deputy nodded, focusing in on the monitor.

'Notice there's no further information on his whereabouts or anything after the date of the trial. And look at the photo at the top.'

Maravich's eyes moved back and forth, up and down. His expression grew grave.

'You're thinking this Warnecke became Ralph Watkins?'

'What do you think?'

'I see a resemblance.'

'There's also this: relocated witnesses are encouraged to choose a new name that has some memory connection to their old one so they're more comfortable with it — perhaps keep the same first name or initials. You'll note this guy's real name was *Raymond* Warnecke. RW.'

'There's no information on this guy after a certain date, and then not long after that, Ralph shows up here in Easton. Okay. That would explain the Marshals.'

'You're being a little coy with me, aren't you? I have a feeling you already know Ralph Watkins had an assumed identity.'

After a moment of silent consideration, the deputy returned Frank's stare and nodded.

'This is still confidential. Rick Casullo told me last night that Ralph was in Witness Protection. That's all he said, though I could tell he was not happy about that, and I shouldn't even be telling you this at all just yet. It'll probably all come out sooner or later.'

Maravich needed an ally, Frank figured. It ran against his grain to be telling what he called stories out of school, but this was his only avenue. And clearly he had decided that Frank could be trusted.

'I had a feeling. You mentioned tracking down Fields' next of kin but haven't yet said a word about doing that for Ralph, and I'd think that would mean more to you. I've been doing some reading this morning on the Federal Witness Security program and there's plenty that's very interesting. Their policy is to inform local law enforcement when a relocated protected witness has been placed in their jurisdiction. Sheriff Casullo had to have known about this, though he might not have seen any reason to make that know-ledge readily known in the Department and most likely didn't like the whole arrange-ment in the least. At this time the Marshals won't want to divulge any more than they have to, but in any case they would have to tell the Sheriff *something* about what's up. And now I'd think the Sheriff would need to bring at least a few of his people up to speed, and you seemed a likely one. It wouldn't surprise me if they kept Ralph's real identity under wraps for a while longer. I'm betting when they do let it out, it's going to be Larry Warnecke.'

A slight smile pulled at the corners of Maravich's mouth.

'Assuming all that is true? It still doesn't mean that Fields was here to kill him.'

'Playing devil's advocate, are you?'

'Someone's got to.'

'Okay. Fair enough. I'll toss ideas out, you shoot them down.'

'Whenever you're ready.'

'There were things that would be consis-tent with Fields coming from the northeast U.S.'

'You mean like the expression he used

for showing an ID. That's thin, don't you think?'

'Taken by itself, maybe. There's his resemblance to a guy I questioned about a suspected murder related to the Boston mob.'

'Again, mighty theoretical. Nothing that would hold up in a courtroom.'

'And the remarkable series of 'accidental' deaths of other individuals who fell afoul of the same mob guy who would have hired him.'

'Also kind of thin.'

' . . . who happened to be an associate of this Pat Fine guy.'

'Nothing here to disprove Fields was what he said he was, though.'

'For Pete's sake, Lee! The guy went out of his way to change his appearance before he left! He shaved his beard, changed his hair color, ditched his glasses!'

Maravich's smile grew a bit deeper.

'You're telling me he shaved and that his glasses were for looks. Maybe he was just vain or a little obsessive about his appearance. Maybe he was a flim-flam artist with that Internet company.'

'He bought whiskey and cigars, consistent with what was found at the scene of Ralph's death, and there was no sign of them around his room, am I right?'

'You're looking at this like a crime scene investigator. I'm looking at it like a prosecutor. 'Consistent' is one thing. 'Conclusive' is another. Any prosecutor around here would laugh me out of his office with that kind of conjecture. Where's the solid evidence?'

'It's the whole picture. All the circumstances around Watkins' death. We've gone over that. He wasn't smoking or drinking anymore, and here he supposedly died by getting drunk and playing with cigars. It wasn't characteristic of him, was it?'

'But you can find people around here who remember that it was. Perhaps not recently, but who's to say his good intentions all went up in smoke?'

'No pun intended, I assume,' Frank remarked.

Maravich chuckled.

'And yet Father McNulty claimed pretty stridently that he felt Ralph's resolution was firm. Did you talk to him last night?'

'As a matter of fact, I did. I got quite a different story from him.'

That stopped Frank in his tracks, just when he was rolling. 'Huh? What do you mean?'

'He said he couldn't be sure just what state of mind Ralph might have been in. He couldn't authoritatively state if Ralph was on the wagon or drinking. That was about all he'd say.'

'You've gotta be kidding!'

The deputy shrugged.

'So at this point all I've got on that is your statement that you heard him claim, in a casual exchange, that he wasn't drinking or smoking anymore. Again, that's not much to hang anything on. There's no evidence of any kind of wrongful death. Nothing that that prosecutor I mentioned would accept and not laugh me out of the office.'

'The priest clammed up! Why would he do that? He was pretty insistent when I spoke with him.'

'Let me ask you something else, Frank. How did you come up with this Warnecke guy to begin with? Where's the connection?'

'I might have mentioned to you earlier, when I stopped at Ralph Watkins' gas station, I had this feeling he looked familiar in some odd way. I couldn't put my finger on it. After I had the same experience with Barry Fields, I just figured I was experiencing away-from-home syndrome, where you want to see something or someone familiar, so your mind starts playing tricks on you, you know?'

'Uh huh. But . . . ?'

'The connection came to me quicker about Fields, and I still think I nailed his identity correctly. Watkins was more subtle. But it was something about his voice, his mannerisms that rang a bell.'

'So you had spoken with this other guy, Warnecke, at some point?'

'No. I watched videos of his testimony.'

'Videos.' Maravich raised his eyebrows. 'You mean like on the news?'

'No. We were looking into the possible connections in the Shumer case I told you about, and a couple of others, with the New England mob. Like I told you before, we don't like wise guys trying to move in from out of town.'

138

'So you were doing research on possible figures involved in the move?'

'Exactly. We consulted with an agent in the FBI's Organized Crime program, a pretty sharp guy named Gary Hedges.'

'Hedges, you say?'

'Right. As in 'trimming'. He provided us with all kinds of background, including on Warnecke and other characters on that scene. We had Federal law enforcement footage on the testimony, among lots of other things. There was just something about the way this Warnecke guy spoke. He was nervous, self-conscious. He kind of twitched his head in odd ways, like an insect.'

Maravich seemed to think of some-thing. He nodded briefly.

'Is that ringing any of those bells with you, Deputy? Sound like Ralph Watkins?'

'Nothing concrete. Just a couple of times I recall he got a little upset about something or other, and he'd get kind of . . . you used the word twitchy?'

Frank nodded. 'You know the feeling you get sometimes about something or somebody. In the police academy they taught me to trust those weird hunches.'

Maravich nodded. 'Me too.'

'Where'd you get your training, if you don't mind my asking?'

'My family's from east Texas and Louisiana. I originally applied to be a Texas state trooper. I trained with them before moving up here.'

'Wow. Big change.'

'Yeah, well, you meet the right person, things happen. Long story. My wife's family is from the next county over, so she had reasons to come back.'

'Sounds to me like the Sheriff was lucky to get you.'

Maravich shrugged.

'Worked out all around.'

'Anyway, that's why I'm pretty sure I zoomed in on Ralph Watkins. I think he's really Larry Warnecke. And I think you can see that and in general you agree with me.'

Maravich folded his arms, pursed his lips and shook his head. 'You might well be right but it's a big leap at this point. You put out a lot of stuff for me here, but it's all conjecture. I'm up against a brick wall. I need something more concrete, Frank.'

'Bricks and concrete. Hard stuff indeed. I'll give you everything I've found. We both understand that's the best I can do. The rest is up to your Department. After this weekend I'll be far away.'

And somehow, he thought but did not say, that was all for the better. He suddenly had the overwhelming urge to be far, far away from Easton.

'Well,' Maravich said, rising from his seat, 'hopefully this will be productive. Thanks for your input, Frank. I need to be getting back out there again.'

'One last question. Yesterday you referred to a case you never closed that hit close to home.'

The deputy nodded.

'If I'm asking anything too personal, feel free to tell me. I was just curious about it.'

Maravich took a deep breath before replying.

'Carla Rae Jordan.'

Frank gave him time.

'We found her behind a road house late

one Saturday night. She had been strangled and left by a garbage hopper. She was twenty-three.'

'Yeah, that sounds like a tough one to deal with. Did you know her? Personally, I mean.'

'Her family. My wife knew them. Not well, but she knew them. Carla Rae was the only child.'

'Nothing panned out? The leads, I mean?'

'Nope. We had a timeline right up to a couple hours before she died, we interviewed all her friends and associates, covered everything. We finally concluded it was someone from out of town just passing through. We checked for similar crimes in surrounding areas, suspicious individuals, all sorts of things. Nothing.' Maravich stared at Frank for a long time. 'In the end, the door started to close. It grew colder and colder.'

Frank nodded. 'I know how that works. Most cases have the best chance of being solved in the first forty-eight hours. You've got a window that lasts a short time and it gets smaller and smaller.'

'Yeah. It's not the only case I ever

worked on that didn't get resolved. It's just the one that still, to this day, rankles my gut the worst.' He shrugged slightly.

'Anyway, from that day forth, I've hated like hell to leave any case unclosed. Guess it's the cop in me.'

'Guess it's the cop in you for sure.'

6

At the rectory of St. Dismas' Church, Frank was directed to a quiet garden in a courtyard, where he found Father Kieran McNulty sitting and reading from a small book — likely saying his daily office. He looked up as Frank approached, closed his breviary and smiled.

'Well, fancy meeting you here.'

'That's the second time I've heard that this morning, Padre.'

'Please, Kieran will do . . . unless you are here for spiritual guidance of some nature.' He gestured for Frank to join him on the oak bench.

'Can't say as that is my reason, Kieran. I'm not really a churchgoing man to begin with.'

'Were you ever? Perhaps you were raised a Catholic?'

'My parents were Dutch Reformed, actually. And not great ones at that.'

McNulty smiled mischievously. 'Then

you're not all that far from a bloody Orange-man. You seem a good sort nonetheless.'

'And you seem all right yourself for what certain relatives of mine would called a Papist. Not a hint of rum or Romanism, much less rebellion.'

'Well, certainly not the rum anymore, at any rate. I've been known to have a rebellious streak. So what brings you here, Frank?'

'I hope I wasn't disturbing your daily office. I can come back.'

'It can keep. The hour's reasonably young.'

'I happened to have a conversation with Deputy Sheriff Maravich this morning. He tells me you recanted on your misgivings about the death of Ralph Watkins.'

'Recanted. Well. You're going to throw the Inquisition at me next, are you? As it happens, I did *reconsider* some of the comments I shared with you yesterday. I saw no reason to make a mountain out of what was not even a molehill.'

'There is a good possibility that Ralph Watkins was living here under an assumed name, that he was a relocated Federal witness, and that all this is going to come out soon.'

McNulty nodded, considering this. 'None of that would change anything.'

'There's a possibility his death was not an accident. And that it's going to be swept under the rug by the Federal authorities.'

'And you're saying that my word could change all that?'

'I don't know, Fath — Kieran. It might make a difference. Don't you want to see a crime recognized and justice met?'

'Tell me, Frank, just for the sake of argument: if Ralph's death were to be determined to be a murder, just who do you think might have been responsible?'

'You know about the guy who showed up the day before, don't you?'

'Oh yes. The poor man met with an unfortunate ending himself, did he not? Shot to death on a lonely road, or so I hear. May his soul rest in peace. And again for that same sake of argument, if he was indeed responsible for someone else's death, wouldn't you say he met a form of justice himself? One that might almost be deemed by some, although not myself, to be divine retribution? At very least, that he met a fate that could not be, shall we say, improved upon by a body of law?'

They sat in silence, looking at each other. There was only the rustling of leaves and the chatter of a squirrel in a nearby tree.

'Kieran, we spoke yesterday about the sanctity of the confessional.'

'Briefly, yes, we did.'

'I find it interesting that Francis Lansdowne wanted to speak with you in the worst way, and now you've changed your mind about all this.'

The priest simply stared at Frank, his expression blank.

'I don't have a particularly deep understanding of how the seal of the confessional works. For the sake of argument, as you say . . . if someone were to confess to you that they had committed a crime, wouldn't you have to divulge that?'

'Solely for the sake of argument?' McNulty shook his head. 'Such a confession would still be a sacred bond. A priest would be strictly bound to say nothing. A priest would strongly urge the penitent to step forward themselves and confess the crime, and to perform whatever restitution was possible to the victims.'

'That would be a very difficult position for a moral man of the cloth.'

'It comes with the job, lad. I'm sure you're familiar with the responsibilities of lawyers and psychiatrists and such. They deal with similar wrenching situations and do so ethically most every day. One such as myself has to answer to a much higher authority in such matters.'

'I seem to recall you told me earlier that Ralph Watkins was not a parishioner here at St. Dismas?'

'Heavens no. He was like yourself, a thoroughly unchurched man, and likely also like yourself, a skeptical sort. That in no way suggests either of you to be anything but ethical and moral, mind you.'

Frank laughed. 'Of course not.'

'I can only tell you this. Ralph and I shared a different bond. I was a counselor of a different sort to him and we shared a different sort of confidentiality.'

'You mean you were his twelve-step sponsor.'

McNulty considered his answer.

'There's no harm, now that he's passed, in shattering that anonymity at least. But whatever was said between us while he lived remains private.'

'A different sort of confidentiality,' Frank repeated. 'He was in the process of making some kind of amends.'

'You seem to know a bit about such things.'

'I've encountered the program many times. Not personally. My job. Friends. You can't avoid it nowadays, can you?'

'These are all interesting conjectures on your part. It's my policy to neither encourage nor discourage such speculations in any way. I'm sure you understand.'

'Father McNulty, remind me never to play poker with you.'

They spoke a bit longer before Frank rose from the bench to make his farewells. McNulty said, 'Might I ask you a question?'

'Sure.'

'Is there a reason you've taken such an interest in the admittedly unusual events of this past week, here in a place a thousand miles from your own home?'

'Good question. I guess I'm just a cop, Kieran. When things don't add up, I just naturally start asking questions.'

McNulty nodded.

'Would you mind if I asked what theory you have about all these things? I'll offer no editorial comment, but simply listen.'

'Why not? Muriel's death strikes me as odd. I have no hard facts on which to base it but I can't help but wonder if someone else was with her when she took that fall off the ladder.'

'Go on.'

'It makes no sense who might have done it. I'm convinced Francis loved her. Everybody in town seems to have loved her. There's nothing concrete to go on.'

'Please continue.'

'As we talked about yesterday, it struck me as odd that Ralph Watkins had gone out of his way to tell me he neither drank nor smoked, and yet he is said to have gotten drunk and accidentally blown up his service station, and himself, by lighting a cigar. The man that I later encountered in the motel, Barry Fields, reminded me of an individual I personally interviewed on the occasion of another suspicious death a few years ago. And I find that Ralph himself had a nagging resemblance to a former mobster who turned evidence and subsequently disappeared. His death brought Federal Marshals, a branch that administers Federal Witness Protection, to Easton. All the roads conceivably lead back one way or another to East Coast crime syndicates. It's all curious to me.'

McNulty waited.

'I'm thinking that this Barry Fields guy was what you might call a hit man, and that he was dispatched to kill Ralph Watkins, which means that his clients had somehow discovered Ralph's true identity in recent days. How and why this happened now, I've got no ideas. I can't see how it would be connected to Muriel's death but if it were my case to investigate, I also couldn't dismiss the idea entirely.'

'And I assume you've told all this to Deputy Maravich.'

'Oh yeah. In great detail.'

'And what does he say about this?'

'In a nutshell, that it's all conjecture,

nothing solid to back up any of it.'

'He strikes me as a good man and a good police officer.'

'I would say so, yes. A very good one.'

'Then I'd say you've suitably discharged your duty, however you might see it.'

'Agreed. I'm going home tomorrow, and whatever comes out of this is out of my hands.' Frank offered a hand to McNulty, who rose to take it. 'I only came here to bury my ex-wife and perhaps bury some ghosts along with her.'

'I would hope you have accomplished that as best you could.'

'I believe I have. It bothers me that there's a possibility the truth may never come out about her death. But in general I've done all I can do.'

'The serenity to accept the things we cannot change, the courage to change what we can, and the wisdom to know the difference,' McNulty mused.

'You seem a very accepting man, Kieran, and a thoughtful one. I'd say those are good qualities in a priest.'

'I'd say they would be good qualities in any walk of life.'

'By the way, it's interesting your parish is named after a thief.'

'I'm impressed you knew that, Frank. Dismas was more than a thief. He was a penitent thief, forgiven by Christ himself from the cross. He stands as a lesson to us all that whatever we do, we are capable of being forgiven, if we repent.' There seemed to Frank to be a deeper and more immediate meaning intended in that.

They shook hands and nodded at one another.

'God speed on your return trip, Frank. I'll remember you in my prayers today.'

'I could probably use them, whether or not I believe in them.'

'It's never a question of whether you believe in the divine, lad. The crux of the matter is that it believes in you.'

★ ★ ★

Frank decided to drive around a bit. Back on the job, that was often how he allowed his mind to work away at cases. He decided to drive out along the highway where Barry Fields had met his death, figuring he'd be able to recognize the scene when he reached it.

He needn't have worried. It was an open stretch of road with mostly farms and a few houses, with few overpasses that were spread apart. About ten miles out of Easton, he saw two overpasses coming up and as he neared them he saw yellow police tape strung around the first.

He slowed as he drove by. There was nobody to be seen, and no other traffic. He pulled over to the side of the road about halfway between the two bridge abutments and stopped his car. He sat thinking for a few minutes. Only two cars passed before he finally got out of the car and walked back towards the first overpass.

When he was near, he stopped and turned to look at the surroundings. The overpasses were less than a hundred feet apart and apparently carried the two lanes of a divided highway. An occasional car or truck would pass by overhead but generally it was quiet. Frank could hear the crunch of his footsteps as he resumed walking toward the abutment.

When he reached the yellow tape that

had been strung around the embankment, he stopped.

Someone could easily drive up from the overhead road and climb down into a position where they could set up a sniper's nest of sorts. He crossed the street, where the opposite abutment had also been cordoned off with yellow tape, and peered over the barrier at the concrete pillars of the bridge. The bridges were relatively new and there wasn't an enormous amount of wear, so he thought it was pretty clear where the bullet hole might be that Maravich had mentioned.

He walked back in the direction of his car, then climbed up the bank until he was in the median between the two lanes of the overhead highway. He could see that not far past the bridges in either direction, the lanes converged more closely. He saw more yellow tape sealing off the bridge area here as well. He stood, hands on hips, for some time, looking at the bridges and thinking.

This didn't strike him as a particularly opportune locale for a professional shooter. Taken along with what Maravich had told him, it certainly seemed that the deputy was right. This was no assassination.

A murder that looked like an accidental death. And now an accidental death that looked like a murder. Could it be?

Frank caught himself in the habitual gesture he always seemed to adopt when he felt puzzled. He was rubbing the back of his neck again. This place was totally crazy.

★   ★   ★

He headed back into Easton and took the road past the Sportsman's Lodge toward Ralph Watkins' service station. He decided it would not be a good idea to stop or even slow down there, lest he run afoul of Deputy U. S. Marshall Candace Maldonado, but he considered it couldn't hurt to drive by at a normal speed and see what there was to see. What remained of the station itself was charred black.

The entire property was cordoned off in more yellow tape. The Marshals' van and sedan were parked off to the side and he could see the crew in jumpsuits, engaged in various activities around the premises. He didn't see Bartolli but did catch a glimpse of Maldonado, standing over a crew member who was squatting down next to the remains of a gasoline pump. There were still a handful of curious pedestrians passing and stopping to peer in at the wreckage.

Frank could swear he still smelled the carbon odors from the fire. He was more familiar with the smells of burned material — and flesh — than he would have liked.

He drove down the street, turned around and drove past one more time, giving the scene a quick look as he passed. He wasn't quite sure why he had wanted to do this. It wasn't his problem to begin with, and he wasn't sure what was to be gained from looking at it in any case. He was just following some intangible urge, he decided.

Maybe just killing time. This place was getting to him and he needed to stay busy until he left tomorrow morning.

So what next? Maybe he could rent a movie back at his motel room, then grab some dinner. Maybe see if Francis would like him to drop by one last time tonight. His mind wandered to their dinner together the previous night. He randomly revisited the meal, their conversation, the house . . .

What suddenly struck him was such a minor detail, but all at once it loomed large.

The things the mind will do, Frank mused, if you leave it alone. The connections it can come up with.

He knew what he'd be doing tonight.

* * *

'Hey, Frank, come on in.' Francis met him at the door with a beer can in his left hand and extended his right to shake.

'Just wanted to come by and say goodbye if you have a few minutes.'

'Sure, sure! Come on in.' Francis shook the can in his hand. It made a shallow sloshing sound. 'I was just going to refresh this. Can I offer you one?'

Frank stepped into the house. 'Actually, if you've got any coffee, that sounds better to me.'

Francis took another look at the beer can in his hand. 'You know, that actually sounds like a better idea. I'm afraid I've been hitting the sauce a bit too much the past few days. Let me go toss this and put up a pot for us. Make yourself at home.' He gestured into the living room. 'I'll be right back.'

Frank found his way back to the same chair he had occupied the previous night and picked up the Lafferty College yearbook from where it still sat on the coffee table. In retrospect, he was surprised it had been left there on the table the past few days.

That had been a mistake.

He paged through to a particular section and scanned several of the pages. He looked up as Francis returned and sat down once again on the couch across from him.

'Coffee'll be ready shortly. So when is your flight out?'

'Tomorrow evening. I'll be leaving in the morning. A couple hours' drive to the airport.'

Francis nodded. 'I guess you had

something of a busman's holiday here, didn't you? I mean, with the deaths and all. Did it make you feel right at home?'

Frank shrugged with a smile. 'Getting back home to work is going to seem pretty pedestrian after all the stuff going on around here.'

'Pretty insane, all right. Did you find out anything else about that guy from the lodge, what might have happened to him?'

'From what the deputy told me, I guess it's all right to tell you. It looks as if it was an accidental shooting. Some kid taking potshots off a bridge late at night. One of them hit that guy.'

Francis' eyes widened for a moment.

'You're kidding!'

'They're looking into a couple of local kids. Lyle and Lem, I think were their names?'

Francis nodded.

'Lloyd Crimmins' kids. I know them. Come to think of it, Lyle's gotten in trouble for shooting at stuff with his air rifle now and then. Broke a few windows more than once. There were like four people in my store repairing their windows one day and talking about it.'

'This was a twenty-two. Sounds like they're really into their guns at that house.'

Francis nodded. 'Lots of hunters and such around here. I stock some rifles and shotguns and ammunition. I've sold a couple of guns to Lloyd and his boys. They go on a lot of hunting trips.'

'I heard something about Lloyd coming back from the Gulf War a little messed up?'

'I've heard the stories too. I've known Lloyd for many years. He's basically a good guy. Something sure seems to have happened to him while he was away. I mean, it's not like he's nuts or anything. He's just a little off in recent years. The kids, though . . . they're kind of sketchy. Their mom's not around anymore and Lloyd, well, I don't think he's doing much in the way of parenting or discipline.'

'The mom died?'

'No, she just left one day a year or so ago. I think she just couldn't take that gang anymore.'

'So the boys are, what, teenagers?'

'Yeah. I'm not sure of their exact ages. Lem's the younger one, he's maybe fourteen? Lyle's about sixteen or seventeen, I'd guess.'

'It would seem one of them is the prime suspect in the shooting at this point. Do me a favor and don't spread that around. I have a feeling the whole story will be coming out soon enough anyway.'

Francis held his hands in the air with a smile. 'Mum's the word from here.' There came a series of beeps from the kitchen. Francis stood up. 'Coffee's done. Be right back. You take anything in yours?'

'Black,' said Frank.

'I should have figured. In the stories, cops always take it black.'

'For once the stories get it right.'

Frank sat back in the chair and folded his arms. He considered exactly how he wanted to broach the next subject. He was still in that pose when Francis returned with two mugs and placed one on the table in front of Frank.

'I'm glad you came here for Muriel,' Francis said as he sat back down.

'Me too. Hey, remember we were talking about your college days and all?'

'Sure. What about 'em?'

Frank picked up the yearbook and paged through it. He looked casual but there was something he was particularly looking for.

'Was this guy a particular friend of yours?' He opened the book and pointed to a photo. Francis leaned over and looked.

'Oh yeah. I knew Pat, sure. Why?'

'You said a couple of guys you knew in school came from families of mobsters, I think you called them. Was this Pat Fine one of them?'

Francis did not answer for a long beat. He just stared first at the book and then up at Frank.

'Why are you asking, Frank?'

'Kind of a coincidence. Just before Ralph Watkins moved here, there was a guy in Boston who turned state's evidence against a prominent organized crime figure named Pat Fine. It says here your friend was from the Boston area. I'm wondering if they were related. If possibly your friend was the son of the other Pat Fine.'

'I suppose it's possible.'

'Come on, Francis. This guy was a friend of yours, wasn't he? You knew the background he was coming out of, didn't you? Why so coy all of a sudden?'

Francis looked down at his coffee cup and said nothing.

'Let me just come out and say all of this. You've been visibly troubled for the past couple of days. I thought that was naturally because of the loss of your wife. But then I got to thinking about it. You seemed better to me the night of the wake. You looked much worse the morning of the burial. That was after word of Ralph Watkins' death had spread. That afternoon you met with Father McNulty for something that seemed to be serious. I'm thinking you suddenly felt guilty about something, that you had something to share in the confessional. Tell me if I'm way off base here, Francis.'

Francis still said nothing, just stared at his coffee cup.

'You told me last night that you hadn't

had any contact with any of your old college buddies in many years. I'm thinking that's not quite true. I'm thinking you had a conversation with your old friend Pat Fine recently. I'm thinking something in that conversation tipped him off to the fact that there might be someone here in Easton that would be of special interest to his family. Both his 'families' actually. Tell me I'm wrong, Francis. Please, tell me I'm wrong, and I'll stop right there.'

Francis finally looked up and, with a sinking feeling, Frank understood that he was not wrong.

'You're thinking it's your fault that the guy who called himself Barry Fields came to town, and that he killed Ralph.'

Francis shook his head and whispered, 'Damn.' A tear swelled in the inner corner of one eye.

'I do not want this to be right, but I'm getting the feeling it is.'

Francis nodded his head.

'Why? How did you figure out who Ralph was and how did you decide to do this?'

'Muriel had him figured out. Well, not

completely, but she had worked out he was from around Boston, a few other things about him. He had said he was here to forget something and just start his life over new. We all respected that. We made some private jokes, when he wasn't around, about Witness Protection, but they were just jokes. Muriel didn't mean any harm. She was just curious. You know how she was. She was trying to figure out how to help him.'

'So Muriel suspected who he really was?'

'She didn't have a name or the exact circumstances or anything like that. But I think she knew enough to make Ralph a little uncomfortable. He was beginning to shy away from her, avoid her. Politely, but it seemed clear he was avoiding her.'

'I'm not quite sure I understand. When did you call your friend about Ralph? Why did you do it?'

Francis stared intently at Frank. 'I called Pat the night that Muriel died. I was convinced that Ralph had killed her.'

The rest of the story took some time to come out with any kind of clarity. Frank was once again going over it with Francis and was finally sipping some of the coffee in his mug.

'I still don't quite get it. You came home from work and found Muriel on the ground outside at the foot of the ladder. How did you conclude that Ralph was responsible?'

'Hell, Frank, I was in shock. You can imagine. Coming home to find the woman you love . . . lying there?'

'I can't imagine. That would be horrible.'

Frank had seen his share of horrors, things that stretched the capacity of the human mind and heart, but he honestly could not imagine himself in a scenario of that kind.

'I was nuts. I called 911. I tried CPR, as well as I know it anyhow. I hoped against hope she wasn't really dead. I desperately prayed that she was still alive somehow.'

'I don't blame you.'

'The cops and EMTs arrived right away and pronounced her dead. There was a big fuss and they took her away and told me there was nothing else I could do that night. After a while I told everyone that I'd be okay and they could leave me. Then I really started going crazy. I poured myself a couple of stiff drinks. All I could think of was that none of this made any sense. First, I felt guilty as hell. She had been nagging me to go up and get that bird's nest and I was all caught up in stuff at work and told her I'd get to it soon enough. It was my fault that she had gone up there. Then I started thinking that it didn't make any sense that she would have done that. She would have waited for someone to be here to hold the ladder for her and help her. Who could that have been? I started building this whole story. It had to have been Ralph. He had come by and innocently volunteered to help her and then knocked her off the ladder. The more I thought about it and the more I drank, the more sense it all made. Around one in the morning, I looked up Pat Fine and made the call. I didn't know who Ralph really could be but I figured he was some kind of witness-protection type from Boston, and I had a suspicion Pat was connected these days. I just was so full of grief that I wanted to get back at him.'

'You never told the police any of your suspicions then.'

'What was I going to tell them? What proof would there have been?'

'Maybe Ralph's fingerprints on the ladder?'

'I never thought of that. Anyway, by the next morning I sure wasn't going to say anything. Not if I had set in motion what I thought I had.'

'You must have had misgivings the next day. Second thoughts.'

'I woke up with a terrible sense of loss of Muriel. The hangover didn't help that any. I didn't give the rest of it much thought that next day. When I finally did, it all seemed unreal. I didn't even believe that my late night call to Pat had any effect. He probably thought I was crazy with grief and drunk when we talked. He likely didn't take me seriously.'

'You didn't make any effort to call off anything you might have put into play?'

'No. I figured that at worst it was a bell

I couldn't un-ring at that point, but that far more likely, nothing would come of it anyway.'

'What did Pat say to you when you told him that story?'

'I don't remember much. He was pretty noncommittal. I did wake him up, it was pretty early in the morning in Boston.'

'He didn't let on that he might be as connected as you suspected? To his father's organization, I mean.'

'No, I don't remember him ever saying anything definite about that. He probably made some disclaimers in fact. I would have expected that. The whole thing seemed so stupid and embarrassing to me later.'

'And then the morning of the burial, you found out that Ralph was killed in a dubious accident.'

'Dubious is the word.' Francis shook his head. 'The worst part? I'm not so sure I really believe he did it any more, killed Muriel I mean. Maybe after all it was just a stupid accident.'

It seemed a very long time that they sat

in silence, drinking from their mugs, not even looking at one another. Somewhere in Francis's house, a clock ticked. In the pall of the house the ticks sounded like crashes.

Finally Francis spoke softly.

'I'm going to turn myself in tomorrow.'

'Did the Padre advise you to do that?'

'Not in so many words. He told me I should follow my conscience. He suggested it might be one course of action.'

Frank did not answer.

'I don't know if I can live with myself if I don't, Frank.'

'I understand. You have to do what you think is right.'

'What if you were in my place, what would you do?'

'Oh damn, I wish you wouldn't ask me something like that. But just some things to think about.'

'Okay.'

'I'm pretty sure that Ralph really was a guy who worked for the Boston mob. If he's who I think he was, he wasn't a good guy by any means. He did a lot of bad stuff in his life. Really bad stuff. He didn't turn on his employers until someone took out his family. And then he went state's evidence and saved his own neck. That's one thing.'

'Are you trying to say he got what he deserved? How could he have deserved to die like that?'

'No, that's not what I'm saying, not at all. I'm saying that he had already set things in motion and for all we know, this is how it had to end for him. Some people would call it karma. Maybe it seems harsh, but that's my perspective from what I do every day. He lived by the sword and he died by the sword.'

Francis didn't seem to have anything to say to that so Frank continued.

'Another thing is, you don't know what happened or how the wise guys found him. I think that by a very strange coincidence, Ralph sent Pat Fine, the father, to Federal prison. He put a lot of Fine's organization on law enforcement radar. Tracking Ralph down and making him pay had to be high on their must-do list. They were already looking for him, and those guys are pretty smart and thorough. You don't know if calling your old friend had any effect or not. You can't be sure your pal was even in his father's business. A lot of that generation, if their parents were in the organization, they wanted to get their kids out of that, into legitimacy. You were in the bag when you called him and woke him up at an ungodly hour, and you don't know whether he even took you seriously. The bottom line, Francis, is that you don't really know if you did anything at all. You don't know if you have any responsibility in this whatsoever.'

Francis nodded somberly.

'Father McNulty said some of the same things.'

'On top of that, Federal Marshals are in town. They've taken over the investigation. They're not happy. The Witness Security Program has never lost a single relocated witness that played by the rules, and these people don't want to become the first, so there's a certain wishful thinking, let's say, that this turns out to be a tragic accident and nothing more. The Sheriff is ticked off at the outsiders coming in, taking over his territory and bringing this catastrophe down upon him, and he's just going to want to see this swept under the rug too. I'm not saying that anyone wants to actively obscure the true story of what may have happened, or necessarily plans to tell any lies. I'm simply saying that there likely isn't going to be any high profile legal action coming out of it. Anything that does result is going to be on the down low, and probably won't involve highly visible prosecutions. So if you feel the right thing is to tell your story, by all means, do so. I am not telling you what to do or not do. But be aware of the context in which your story's going to be received. Be ready to have it met with some skepticism.'

Francis digested all of that quietly.

'One further thing. If you do come forward on this, I'd suggest you talk to Deputy Lee Maravich. And I strongly suggest that you do *not* mention my name in any of this.'

'Do you think they're going to think I'm crazy?'

'Maravich won't. Someone might try to

make *you* think you are. But that's not why you want to come forward, is it?'

Francis simply shook his head.

Frank thought about the need to remove the burden of guilt, what power it could hold. His past few days, he realized, had been filled with it.

He thought about Kieran McNulty, carrying so much, not just in his role as a father confessor but also as a twelve-step sponsor. He couldn't imagine shouldering that much of a burden of confidentiality.

'You know what's funny?' Francis said quietly.

'No, what?'

'Pat called me Frank. That's how he remembered me. I said 'This is Francis Lansdowne' and he said, 'Hey, Frank! What's up?' It was like I was back in the old school days, like all the years in between had never happened. I was Frank again.'

'So here we are. Two Franks.'

'That's what Muriel used to say. She had a fondness for Franks. She'd kid me when she'd refer to you, you were the Other Frank.'

'At least she didn't call you the other one.'

Frank laughed despite himself.

'Waiter, two Franks, please.'

Francis actually cracked a weak smile. 'And hold the mustard.'

7

Frank had dropped his bag into the trunk of the rental car and closed the trunk when he saw the deputy, in uniform, standing near the front of his car, arms folded across his chest.

'Morning. I was hoping I'd catch you before you left.'

'Don't they ever give you a day off, Deputy?'

'They got me on a lot of overtime this week, what with all that's been going on. My wife's not happy that I couldn't join her at church this morning.'

'I'll bet she'll be less unhappy when that overtime pay comes in your envelope.'

'Good point. I have to believe you're happy to be getting away from all this mess and leaving it to us.'

'You keep telling me this isn't how things usually are around here, but I'm beginning to have my doubts. I'm looking forward to returning to the usual straightforward murders and muggings back home.'

Maravich laughed.

'Honest to God, this is usually a quiet town, downright boring.'

'How are things working out with the shooting?'

'We got prints off of Barry Fields and sent them out to the FBI's database and so forth. So far nothing's come back. We're still trying for an ID of some kind. His company's a dead end and there so far aren't any other viable leads, next of kin, anything like that. The actual shooting, pretty much like we expected. The ballistics matched up to Lemuel Crimmins' gun. The other evidence played out the same way, the shoe print, the fingerprints, the whole nine yards. We found a witness who saw his father Lloyd's pickup truck on the divided overpass highway that night. Lem's pretty much owned up to being out there, taking potshots at passing cars for a couple of nights. He must have realized that he hit Fields. It seems he picked up and took off in a hurry right after that.'

'He's just a kid, right?'

'Not even fifteen.'

'Pretty messed up. His life's never going to be the same.'

'I have to say, some of us saw it coming. But you're right, it's a shame. Maybe this will serve as a wakeup call for Lloyd. Maybe he'll get some help for himself, and maybe at least Lyle's still got a chance.'

'Redemption,' Frank muttered. There seemed to be a lot of people seeking it or needing it here this week.

'Speaking of redemption, I had a visit earlier this morning from Francis Lansdowne.'

'Really?'

'He told me quite a story. I have a feeling you might know something about it already.'

'I'm just a visitor, getting ready to go home.'

'Uh-huh. He claims he made a phone call that might have set things in motion, Barry Fields and the fire and all.'

'And why would he do that, exactly?'

'He claims that he thought Ralph might have killed Muriel.' Maravich eyed Frank carefully.

'Why would Ralph kill Muriel?'

'Because he thought that Muriel had figured out who he really was.'

'Really. Do you put any stock in that?'

'Can't say as I do. The story he told me is pretty convoluted. A lot of ifs and maybes. I'm not even sure how we can look into it. On top of that, it's a big stretch for me to believe that Ralph Watkins would have killed Muriel Lansdowne. Even Francis wasn't sure he really believed it in the end.'

'And what does Sheriff Casullo think of it?'

'I haven't broached it with him as yet. He gets to sleep in late this morning and come in in the afternoon. I doubt he'll welcome this development. I'm not yet sure what I'm going to tell him — or not.'

'What about the Marshals? Are they still around?'

'I think they cleared out last night or earlier today. I don't see their vehicles here.'

They both glanced around at the basically empty parking lot. 'The Bobbsey Twins stopped in at the station last night for another high-level get-together with Rick Casullo.'

'The Bobbsey Twins. Good name for them.'

'I have still not been privy to any of those conferences. I have a feeling he's going to give us the word later today or tomorrow.'

'You're thinking that the powers that be want this case closed.'

'I am thinking that, yes.'

'But you don't.'

'I do not. But I'm not sure what my options are at this point.'

'You're a good cop, Lee. You're going to do the right thing, but you also know exactly what you're up against.'

'To be honest, right now I'm not sure what I think I ought to do.'

'Hey, I've told you, I hate it when Federal or state authorities come in and step on my business, and I really hate it when wise guy types come in from out of town to pollute my home turf. We've got a hard enough job under normal circumstances, without all this outside nonsense. I definitely get it. And when something's unsettled, it stays up there in my head as well. I get all that, I really do.'

Maravich nodded solemnly. 'But you gotta know when to hold 'em and when to fold 'em.'

'Exactly.' Frank put his hand out. 'Drop me a line sometime, let me know how you came out of all this.'

Maravich shook his hand firmly. 'I'll do that, Detective. Thanks for the conversations.'

'It's been a pleasure, Lee.'

'Same here. Safe journey home. Vaya con Dios, as we say back in Texas.'

'It's funny, there's something the Padre said to me.'

'Which was?'

'Something to the effect that it's never a question of whether God's with you but whether you're with God. Or maybe that's just how I interpreted it.'

'Yeah, that sounds like the Padre all right. Eternal optimist, huh?'

'Frankly, Lee, unless he's a vigilante at heart, I'm not seeing the hand of God very much in the proceedings of this week.'

Maravich nodded slowly and somberly. 'Hard to be like the Padre if you're a cop.'

Frank traced a benediction in the air. 'Amen to that, brother.'

* * *

As Frank drove along the highway, his head still buzzed with all the elements of the crazy story in which he had lived for the past few days.

Protected Federal witness in a new identity. Mob hit man. Murder made to look like a fluke accidental death. In a bizarre twist, a fluke accidental death that looked like a murder.

Possibly — just possibly — his ex-wife, playing detective, getting herself killed.

A blooming cover up by Federal authorities with the coerced complicity of the local Sheriff.

The taste it all left in his mouth was at least as bad as anything he had ever experienced in Personal Crimes.

Before he knew it, the hours had slipped away, the secondary road had brought him to the Interstate, and he was on the exit ramp for the airport. He hardly remembered any of it.

★   ★   ★

It was over two weeks later when the mail cart passed through the unit and the duty officer dropped his mail on his desk. There was a large manila envelope on top, hand-lettered with a familiar return address. He ripped it open and pulled out a folded-up section from a Midwestern newspaper. A yellow Post-It note was stuck onto the first page with a two-word printed message in the same hand as the address: THERE'S MORE.

Lee Maravich.

Frank shook his head and smiled.

He opened it up and read the headline to the article.

EXISTENCE OF A PROTECTED MOB
WITNESS SHOCKS A SMALL TOWN

A subhead read: TWO BIZARRE DEATHS
FOUND TO BE UNRELATED.

The muddled mystery that has baffled a small town for the past ten days seems to finally be coming to a head with new official disclosures.

A spokesperson for the U.S. Marshals Service today confirmed that a man who died in a service station fire last week in the township of Easton had in fact been living under an assumed identity as part of the Federal Witness Security Program.

Raymond Lawrence 'Larry' Warnecke, a longtime member of New England organized crime, whose crucial prosecution testimony cemented the case against mob boss Pat Fine, was relocated to Easton three years ago and was living under the assumed identity of Ralph Leonard Watkins, the proprietor of Ralph's Automotive Services.

Deputy U.S. Marshal Candace Maldonado affirmed Warnecke's true identity and said that he had been established in the area with the knowledge, consent and cooperation of local law enforcement.

Some questions had been raised,

Maldonado further explained, regarding the circumstances around Warnecke's death, but these had been carefully and thoroughly investigated and the Marshals Service was now completely satisfied that the tragic explosion and fire were the result of an accident. She pointed out that the U.S. Marshals' Service has an unblemished record of protection of its charges when they have cooperated with the requirements of the program, and that this case was no exception.

Freeman County Sheriff Richard Casullo confirmed Maldonado's statement, including that he had been made aware of Warnecke's true identity and had been consulted prior to the relocation, but declined to expand upon that.

Frank shook his head as he continued to read the remainder of the article. There was no mention of Barry Fields' presence or death. It was as if the question of Fields' possible involvement in the death of Ralph Watkins was never even a consideration. He could imagine Lee Maravich's reaction to all this. He wondered what the 'more' promised by the sticky-note could be.

It wasn't long before his questions were answered.

Later that same day Frank received a call.

'Detective Vandegraf, this is FBI Special Agent Gary Hedges. Possibly you remember me.'

'Agent Hedges. Of course I do. The Shumer case.'

'I happen to be in town right now. Might I be able to meet with you?'

'As a matter of fact, I'm about to grab some lunch. Can you join me?'

'Actually, this is business and I'm on a deadline. How about I bring us up some sandwiches, might there be somewhere private we can talk there?'

★ ★ ★

Frank was able to commandeer an interview room, basically a bare-walled chamber badly in need of a paint job with nothing but a metal table and chairs, and apologized for the spartan amenities.

Hedges waved it off. He was a tall, broad-shouldered man and looked to have aged considerably since the last time they had met a couple of years previously.

Hedges came bearing a large paper bag and a briefcase. They sat and Hedges handed him a wrapped sandwich and a container of coffee. 'Hope you don't mind if we eat while we talk. I'm on a flight in a few hours and I need to make every minute count. Nice place you suggested for the grub, by the way. The Reubens look good.'

'Their coffee is better than ours too,' Frank said happily. As Feds went, Hedges was about as decent as they came, and more than a little unorthodox at times. Generally Personal Crimes was not delighted to deal with the Bureau, but a little bit of good personal history went a long way.

'Appreciate this. So what can I do for you, Agent?'

'Call me Gary, okay?' Somehow Hedges managed to simultaneously unwrap his sandwich while snapping open his brief-case and removing a Manila folder, which he slid across the table to Frank. He was definitely not your stereotypical Bureau agent, Frank mused. But he had learned that the guy's quirkiness masked an almost scary sharpness and tenacity.

Everything was to a purpose.

'This guy in this file. Look familiar to you?' He said it as he bit into the Reuben.

Frank opened the file and stared at two four-by-five-inch photographs clipped to a typed report with a very familiar format.

'This looks like Artie Burns.'

Hedges took another bite, put down the sandwich, and simply nodded.

Frank scrutinized the face in the photos. 'He looks a little different in these photos, the hair and the clean-shaven face, and he's a bit younger, but I'd say it's him, sure.'

'I believe you also know him by another name as well.'

'You don't mean . . . ?'

'Barry Fields?'

Now it was Frank's turn to simply stare. It made sense, of course. It was just a surprise to hear anyone else accepting it.

Hedges smiled and pointed to the report. 'I don't think it will come as any surprise to you, neither of those is his real name. Or was.'

'They must have run a fingerprint check,' Frank said. 'The Sheriff's Department in Easton.'

'IAFIS. You can read the report right there.'

Frank scanned the stapled sheets. The Bureau's Integrated Automated Fingerprint Identification System — IAFIS — was the largest criminal fingerprint base in the world, and also included millions of civil prints. It was available to law enforcement throughout the country. Of course someone would have sent a set of Fields's prints to the database for comparison.

'Mitchell Gravell?' Frank read the name off the page.

'That's how we've got him in the system.'

'How did you happen to make the connection and jump on this? I mean, *you*, personally?'

'Well, now, that's an interesting story. I was contacted by a Sheriff's Deputy from out there in Freeman County. He asked for me specifically.'

'Let me guess. Lee Maravich.'

Hedges' manner turned serious. 'This is strictly between you and me now.' Frank nodded in agreement. 'We had a most interesting conversation, let me tell you.'

'Unbelievable. I only briefly mentioned you in passing when we were talking. Lee's a sharp cookie.'

'He provided me with enough to run with. I started retracing some of the other accidents we suspected were hit jobs. So far I can't definitely establish this guy's presence at the time and place of any of them, but there are some interesting coincidences that are turning up. They're still long shots but with some more hard work, we might just start to make some inroads on those connections. This guy's good. Or he was. He avoided trouble. But everybody makes a mistake sooner or later.'

Frank continued to read over the report sheets. 'Vagrancy in some small town in Eastern Shore Maryland? You gotta be kidding me. That's his entire rap sheet?'

'Something must have gone bad and he was trying to make it back to his home base, which we believe to be New England. A fluke of luck. Nobody would ever have picked up on this if he hadn't gotten himself killed. He would have been buried in the cracks of the system forever.'

'So what do you need from me?'

Hedges smiled.

'I need you to help me with the one case I think I can definitely pin on our friend here and begin to trace it back to the Organization. Larry Warnecke. I believe you know the name?'

'I was led to believe that case has been closed by the Marshals.'

'Yes, well . . . they would *like* for that case to be closed. The Bureau feels a little differently about it.'

Frank envisioned a very, *very* unhappy Deputy Marshall Maldonado. The image was not entirely unpleasant to him. But it had its downside.

'You're dropping me right into the middle of an interagency squabble, it sounds like.'

Hedges put up a hand. 'Your name is never even going to come up in this. Officially, all we are discussing here today is the case we originally conferred on, the Lon Shumer murder. The entire reason I'm here is to confer on background and information on your case, which I hope we can do in detail. And I think you can look forward to our unearthing considerably more on that before we are finished. But on this other matter . . .'

Hedges paused to consider his words. 'Just between you and me and nobody else. You were there. Maybe you feel that justice has not been served, as does another individual who shall also remain unnamed.'

Frank shook his head. 'You could get Lee in a hell of a lot of trouble, Gary. And me too.'

'Do me a favor, Frank — just tell me what you know. I'm going to keep both your names totally out of this, you have my solemn word, and I hope we've got sufficient history that that means something to you. But I need to have some plausible springboard from which to launch my investigation.'

He reached over his sandwich into the briefcase and pulled out a pencil and a notebook. 'No recordings. All handwritten. We all want the same thing here. There's a lot of wise guys I've been after who think they've gotten away scot-free with all kinds of mischief, and I want them in the worst way. There's potential here for us to take down a lot of them, to clear a lot of open cases we thought were hopeless for once and for all. Please, help me out.'

Frank considered for a long moment and weighed the pros and cons. Lee Maravich had shown some guts in contacting Hedges. It was clear the truth meant a lot to him in the scheme of things. He couldn't leave him hanging out on that limb by himself.

But he didn't have to tell it all. He never mentioned anything about Francis.

8

It was two days later, as he was grabbing his car keys and preparing to head out the door on a fresh call, when Frank's old-style flip cell phone started buzzing in his pocket. He fished it out and answered it, gruff and a bit impatient.

'Frank Vandegraf.'

'Lee Maravich here.'

'Lee! What's up?' Frank dropped his keys back on the desk and plopped himself into his chair. The murder call could wait a couple of minutes, he reflected. Everybody was already dead there. Nobody was going anywhere.

'Got a minute?'

'Why not? You seem to be trying to get us both in a heap of trouble these days.'

'Listen to you. 'Heap of trouble'? That your idea of sounding like a Texas boy?'

'Seriously, Lee. Special Agent Hedges came into town the other day, just to talk with me about all sorts of things. I'm sure you're the one who put him up to that. I'm amazed you remembered his name. I only mentioned him once.'

'Sometimes, I'm not such a bad cop, Frank.'

'So, to what do I owe the honor of this call?'

'I promised I'd keep you in the loop. Thought you'd be interested in recent developments.'

'Go ahead.'

'I found reason to go back and check a few things around Francis Lansdowne's house. Happened to pull some prints off his ladder. Even with it having been touched and moved around some more in the past couple weeks, would it surprise you to learn that it held a few fingerprints belonging to that Warnecke fellow, or should I say Ralph Watkins? On top of that, Francis told me there was never a time in his memory that Ralph had ever been at his house, so that led from one thing to another.'

'How did you get the Sheriff to go along with that one?'

'Um, I sort of didn't. It happened to

come up on a day while Rick Casullo was on a fishing trip. Just sort of a coincidence.'

'Uh huh. Astounding coincidence. And how did Sheriff Casullo react when he found out you had done that?'

'I put the whole thing together and presented it to him as a fait accompli. Did you know Texas boys said stuff like that, 'fait accompli'?'

'I do now.'

'Anyway, I had a chance to think it out and suggest a way he could announce all this and make himself look good, so he kinda forgave me.'

'Better to beg for forgiveness than to ask for permission,' Frank recited.

'Rule to live by. Heard that a bit in my stint in Texas. Anyhow, by another strange coincidence, this all went down just as Special Agent Hedges arrived and began his own investigation into the death of Watkins — I mean Warnecke. Whoever.'

'For a man who doesn't believe in coincidences, you are up to your ears in them all of a sudden.'

'Funny thing, isn't it? Well, that was

still another matter that had come up to irritate Rick Casullo, and I just sorta suggested a way to make lemonade out of all these lemons falling on his head.'

'What's the bottom line on all this? Is Francis going to be involved in any of it?'

'Nope. I never mentioned his little confession to the Sheriff or anybody else. Kinda saw no reason to. As far as anybody else knows, the evidence that Warnecke might have killed Muriel came as a shock to Francis. Your bottom line is that Warnecke crossed the line and committed a murder, and now there's reason to believe he wasn't exactly toeing the line to begin with. Maybe he cut a few other corners and broke a few other laws while he was living in Easton. There's sufficient doubt so that they can paint him as a rogue in the Program. The Marshals can make a case that their Witness Security Program record is still unblemished in cases where the subject played by the rules, so they are now publicly cooperating with the FBI to establish the truth about Barry Fields and the death of Larry Warnecke.'

'Sounds too neat to be for real.'

'So far, so good, Frank. Casullo's on board and it might just play out for the best. He's no fan of the Bobbsey Twins since they originally dropped this whole Witness Protection thing in his lap, and he's kinda pleased that in private they're gnashing their teeth over these developments. The Sheriff does like his payback.'

'I'm glad Francis can be kept out of this.'

'No need to bring him in. There's only three of us, including Francis himself, who know the real story about his involvement, and none of us seem predisposed to telling it.'

Four, thought Frank, but the Padre wasn't about to say anything either.

Lee Maravich, apparently nowhere near the straight arrow he had presumed, continued to surprise him. He was beginning to remind Frank of some of the hard-boiled protagonists in the noir crime dramas Muriel loved: principled but starkly realistic guys who weren't beyond bending a rule to see real justice done.

'It looks as if Hedges might be tracing

that Fields character back to some other hits as well,' Frank continued, 'including our cold case on Lon Shumer. We might yet close that one, even if we don't end up with any official credit, which is a real possibility. Hedges is a good man in my estimation, but the Feds are great at hogging the spotlight. What we might be able to take from this is some closure anyway, knowing that our instincts were right, and that the killers didn't get away after all.'

'You and I both know we might not get out of this exactly how we'd like to, right?'

'Seldom do, Lee, in my experience.'

'Mine as well, Frank, but let's hope for the best. Well, just thought I'd bring you up to speed. And fact be known, I do think everything's going to turn out just fine. Keep your fingers crossed. The game's afoot.'

'Damn, do they say that in Texas too?'

'Picked that up from some English guy somewhere, as I recall.'

'Keep in touch, Deputy. It's been a pleasure working — well, officially not working — with you. Watch your back.'

'Vaya con Dios, Detective. Hasta la vista.'

Frank hung up and reached for his car keys once again.

It was better than he had expected, if not as good as he had hoped.

Strangely, he felt a little lighter as he stood up and headed for the door. In the corridor, he passed a glum-looking Marlon Morrison, who shot him an odd look.

'Hey, what the devil are you so happy about all of a sudden, Frank?' He moved on without waiting for a reply, grumbling to himself beneath labored breath.

Frank realized he must be smiling, and that perhaps he hadn't done much of that in the past few days.

As good a time to move on as ever.

We do hope that you have enjoyed reading this large print book.

Did you know that all of our titles are available for purchase?

We publish a wide range of high quality large print books including:
Romances, Mysteries, Classics General Fiction Non Fiction and Westerns

Special interest titles available in large print are:
The Little Oxford Dictionary Music Book, Song Book Hymn Book, Service Book

Also available from us courtesy of Oxford University Press:
Young Readers' Dictionary (large print edition) Young Readers' Thesaurus (large print edition)

For further information or a free brochure, please contact us at:
**Ulverscroft Large Print Books Ltd., The Green, Bradgate Road, Anstey, Leicester, LE7 7FU, England.
Tel:** (00 44) **0116 236 4325
Fax:** (00 44) **0116 234 0205**

DARK JOURNEY

Catriona McCuaig

Midwife Maudie Bryant is used to stumbling across murder — but now that she is the mother of a little boy, she has vowed to leave any future crime-solving to her husband Dick, a policeman. However, death strikes too close to home when a wealthy local woman, Cora Beasley, is found strangled with a belt from Maudie's dress. To make matters worse, it is well known that Maudie believed 'the beastly woman was out to snare Dick'. Can Detective Sergeant Bryant help to solve the crime before Maudie is charged as a suspect?

SHERLOCK HOLMES VS. FRANKENSTEIN

David Whitehead

An intriguing mystery lures Sherlock Holmes from the comfort of Baker Street in the winter of 1898: the ghastly murder of a gravedigger in the most bizarre of circumstances. Soon Holmes and Watson are travelling to the tiny German village of Darmstadt, to unmask a callous killer with an even more terrifying motive . . . In nearby Schloss Frankenstein, the eponymous family disowns the rumours attached to its infamous ancestor. But the past cannot be erased, and an old evil is growing strong once again — in the unlikeliest of guises . . .

THE RADIO RED KILLER

Richard A. Lupoff

Veteran broadcaster 'Radio Red' Bob Bjorner is the last of the red-hot lefties working at radio station KRED in Berkeley. His paranoia makes him lock his studio against intruders while he's on the air — but his precaution doesn't save him from a horrible death that leaves him slumped at the microphone just before his three o'clock daily broadcast. Homicide detective Marvia Plum scrambles to the station to investigate. Who amongst the broadcasters, engineers, and administrators present at the station was the murderer — and why?

THE BIG FELLOW

Gerald Verner

Young Inspector Jim Holland of Scotland Yard is under particular pressure to bring to justice 'The Big Fellow' — the mastermind behind a gang committing ever more audacious outrages. As the newspapers mount virulent attacks on Scotland Yard for failing to deal with the rogues, and the crimes escalate from robbery to brutal murder, Holland finds not only his own life threatened, but also that of his theatre actress girlfriend, Diana Carrington.

BLING-BLING, YOU'RE DEAD!

Geraldine Ryan

When the manager of newly-formed girl band Bling-Bling needs a Surveillance Operator to protect them, retired policeman Bill Muir jumps at the chance — but he doesn't know what he's let himself in for . . . In *Making Changes*, Tania Harkness is on a mission to turn around her run-down estate. But someone else is equally determined to stop her . . . And in *Another Country*, Shona Graham returns to her native Orkney island of Hundsay to put right a wrong that saw her brother ostracised by the community many years perviously . . .

THE DOPPELGÄNGER DEATHS

Edmund Glasby

While investigating a fatal car crash, Detective Inspector Vaughn's interest is piqued when forensic evidence points to murder, and he is shown the eerie antique doll found sitting on the passenger seat. The blood-spattered doll bears an extraordinary resemblance to the dead man, and on its lap is an envelope containing the message: 'One down. Five to go.' When a second doll is discovered beside another murder victim, the desperate race is then on to find and stop the killer from completing the set of six murders . . .